Michael Cook is a forme
charity but now concen
English and began by wr
first full length critical
followed by a discuss
detective fiction and the ghost story.

Drawing on these themes, he has now started writing fiction which combines the supernatural with rational inquiry. His first such collection of tales, a novel and three short stories, *'The Librarian & other strange stories'*, introduced Jack Tregarden, an antiquarian, recounting his first disturbing case. *The Hexagon* is the second Tregarden novel in the trilogy, set some two years after *The Librarian* and continuing the incredible story of his association with the de Betancourt family.

Michael Cook lives with his wife and a three-legged cat in the Blackdown Hills.

Also by Michael Cook:

The Librarian & Other Strange Stories (2017)

Non-Fiction:

Narratives of Enclosure in Detective Fiction: The Locked Room Mystery (Palgrave Macmillan, 2011)

Detective Fiction and the Ghost Story: The Haunted Text (Palgrave Macmillan, 2014)

The Hexagon

Part Two
of the Tregarden Ghost Trilogy

Michael Dodsworth Cook

Published by Belvin Water Books

ISBN 978-1-83853-980-1

Cover Design by Footfall Events & Marketing
http://footfallevents.com

Belvin Water Books, 2021

Acknowledgements

My thanks in particular go Will Broadfoot at Footfall for the excellent cover design. As ever I am indebted to Jenny, my wife and the whole family for their constructive criticism, encouragement and endless patience.

Author's Preface

This is the second book in the Tregarden series and is, in every sense, a sequel to *The Librarian* which introduced the character of Jack Tregarden, the antiquarian. A third book is planned.

Michael Cook

website: http://www.michaelcookonline.com
I am also on Twitter: @MichaelDodCook

In memory of Ebony

The H⬡xagon

"The dark side of life, and the horror of it, belonged to a world that lay remote from his own select little atmosphere of books and dreamings."

Algernon Blackwood

Foreword

It has now been nearly three years since I presented the details of the affair at Ashcombe Abbey, which was published under the title 'The Librarian' on behalf of my late father, Jack Tregarden. At that time I indicated that further episodes from his life would be forthcoming. Having examined more of his papers, I now realise that 'The Librarian' is just the first in a trilogy of linked stories. 'The Hexagon' is the second part set some two years after his first encounter with the supernatural world.

My role in producing these manuscripts is minimal; my father left each one as a final draft ready for publication, as was always his habit. I have merely acted as a go-between for the dead and the living. My father knew that the sharing of these experiences with a wider audience would inevitably embarrass some very well-known and influential people but, nevertheless, he felt that these incredible stories should not languish in darkness but be brought into the light. I agree with him.

Charles Tregarden
2021

Prelude

In the days after the affair at Ashcombe Abbey it seemed I went as a ghost, I thought as a ghost, I acted as a ghost and the animus which gave my life purpose had all but deserted me. The husk of my being allowed me little more than the pursuance of the most mundane routine as if anything which required reason or judgement was now beyond me. I was lost to the world.

Yet, curiously, this dislocation was the means by which a sense of self-awakening grew within me. It is true, of course, that the particular memory of events in that dreadful oubliette beneath the library continued to haunt me and perhaps my withdrawal was a natural, if transitory, defence against such trauma. More fundamental to my whole being, greater even than Simon's apparent betrayal was the realisation that the supernatural, which I had always dismissed as sheer fantasy, may well exist after all. Imagine what such a revelation meant to an academic like me who had spent his life in pursuit of verifiable truth. What unnerved me as a historian was the possibility that a whole unseen history existed, one which was acted out even as we went about our daily lives.

As I was recovering at Ashcombe following the trauma of Simon's death, echoes of the past, which I thought had been exorcised, resounded once more. The days during this period I spent in a state of listless inactivity. I felt quite unable to concentrate on even the most trivial matters, let alone my own research. Curiously, the one thing that did capture my attention was a task given to me by Simon's sister, Em, and that was to collate her brothers personal papers, with special reference to anything that might relate to the library. Simon had mentioned to me that he was in the process of making further acquisitions and the idea was that I could take this forward as time went by. Call it a kind of cathartic therapy if you like. To my surprise, it worked. Given the extraordinary circumstances of our final encounter you could be forgiven for thinking that this was the last thing on earth I needed, and, at first, I resisted. But I came to see that this would give me an opportunity to complete the closure of Simon's affairs and draw a line under our strange relationship. By this time, Em and I were growing closer, the bond strengthened no doubt by the mutual loss we had suffered. This meant that I was trusted to use my discretion in matters of this kind.

The first time I entered his office at Ashcombe after his death it seemed inconceivable that we had buried him just two weeks ago, but that he lived on and had merely stepped out for a brief moment soon to return. There was an intense feeling of his presence which I could not shake off. But as the days went by, I immersed myself in the work, sifting through the papers; some were routine mundane matters of housekeeping either for Em's attention or to be sent to the family solicitor and, once I had assigned these, I was left with a pile of correspondence relating to acquisitions. Simon had been as good as his word to me when we had discussed the future of the library during his final days. The Ashcombe library was already famed for its repository of medieval and renaissance works but Simon's focus had shifted to more recent masterpieces. It seemed he was already in negotiations to bring a copy of The Subscribers' Edition of T E Lawrence's

Seven Pillars of Wisdom produced in 1926 with a limited print run of about 200 copies, each with a unique, sumptuous, hand-crafted binding. Other gems in the pipeline included first editions of Freud, the four collections of *Ghost Stories of an Antiquary* by M R James, the irony of which did not escape me, and a signed copy of Mary Shelley's *Frankenstein*. This last was published by a small London publishing house of Lackington, Hughes, Harding, Mayor, & Jones in 1818. Just five hundred copies of this seminal book were produced, and many had been lost. It seemed that while Simon had benefitted little from his family inheritance the Library Trust Fund was in an extremely healthy state and ran into many millions.

In the course of the next few months I would be able to take forward some of these enlightened transactions, and in many ways, they seemed a fitting memorial to Simon, who, despite the contortions of his final days and his unaccountable behaviour, had always loved books. After a few days I had, as far as I was able, dealt with all the outstanding business, passing on any requests for funding to the trustees who held the purse strings. Although access to the library was strictly limited, there were constant requests from many of the leading academics of the day and because of its importance there was an obligation on the trustees to grant such requests.

With most of the immediate tasks completed, I sat back with a sigh thinking that my assignment was coming to an end.

If I had left things there, I would have missed it.

Free from the rigour of paperwork I studied Simon's desk properly for the first time; it was an elegant eighteenth-century mahogany affair with a kneehole design. On either side of the sitter were two sets of three drawers; in the interests of thoroughness I thought I should check the contents, without expecting to find anything of importance. Five of the drawers opened with an effortless swish, the lowest drawer on the left-hand side, however, would not open; it was clearly locked for some reason. This was now the last outpost of resistance, and although I told myself that it really did not matter, my frustration grew into a nagging curiosity. I had been unable to find the key and as the time went by, I began to wonder what it could be that was so important as to warrant such security. None of the keys on his regular key ring fitted the rather old-fashioned lock and the missing item was nowhere to be found in the desk itself or anywhere in Simon's effects. I could not even access this from above as each drawer was lined. Neither Em nor any other member of the household could shed any light on the whereabouts of the missing key. After the events in the library I felt a germ of anxiety grow in my mind; forbidden spaces and their contents now held concerns that hitherto I had never experienced. A week went by and my searches turned up nothing.

One day, when I had all but given up my quest, I sat again at the desk contemplating the problem. I could, of course, just force the lock and open the drawer that way, or rip open the lining, but I recoiled immediately from such an idea. The desk itself was a valuable antique, such an act would have been sheer vandalism. But more than the physical violation, it seemed to me a desecration of Simon's memory and an act of intellectual laziness. I was sure that Simon had hidden the key somewhere and, in that place, it was there to be discovered. If I could not find the key, I was not entitled to see the contents of the drawer. I tried to put myself in Simon's shoes and imagine where he might conceal something which was clearly important to him. An uneasy thought came into my head. What if he had it placed somewhere in the library? A cold sweat took hold of me, I had not been anywhere near the library since the fateful night and the thought of navigating its aisles again filled me with utter dread.

This rising anxiety was not helping with my search, so to clear my mind I decided instead to focus on the surroundings and happier memories of my late friend. Apart from Simon's working desk his elegant office contained the familiar paraphernalia of a well-to-do gentleman's place of work. To my right (as I sat at his desk) stood a Wellington alongside an attractive drop leaf table from the eighteenth century, on which lay an assortment of files and documents, most of which I had already examined. On my left a large bookcase contained a personal selection of Simon's favourite literature sitting rather self-consciously with assorted reference books on furniture, finance and business practice. Together with a fine collection of prints which adorned the walls, the whole room made for the most comfortable of places in which to work. But of all the contents of that office it was that which faced the desk that transfixed me. Broken only by the door in one corner, this wall contained the most singular combination of artefacts in the whole of Ashcombe.

Whenever I had visited the office, I invariably had my back to this space, facing Simon at his desk. Sitting opposite now gave me the opportunity to consider this curious sight at length. There stood a particularly fine Louis XIV *escritoire*, placed in the centre of the wall bathing in the light from the window behind me. Everything about the piece exuded quality: the exquisite marquetry, its design resplendent in different species and colours of wood; the beautifully worked cabriole legs and the impeccable lines of the overall design led me to believe that it could be by Pierre Golle himself. In the tradition of furniture from the *haute époque,* this was a desk to admire, more than to use. As if this was not enough, Simon had told me that the piece was given to a de Betancourt from the French branch of the family as a wedding gift from the Sun King himself. How it had ended up at Ashcombe goodness only knows but it had originally adorned a drawing room in the august surroundings of the

Palace of Versailles, demonstrating, if it was necessary, the exalted connections of this extraordinary family.

As I gazed on this extravaganza my mind wandered to the court of Louis and the dazzling spectacle of this period of overindulgence (for some) and the elaborate art that it produced. A piece of this provenance deserved at the very least a Rigaud portrait as a companion piece to complement its magnificence, but counterintuitively, staring down unapologetically from above was a likeness of Edgar Allan Poe! It was an enlarged print from the familiar 1849 Daguerreotype but alongside its dazzling neighbour this somewhat dowdy representation paled somewhat. In fact, knowing Simon, this juxtaposition did not altogether surprise me; he had been an aficionado of Poe the whole time I had known him. The obvious and deliberate incompatibility of the portrait and the *escritoire* would no doubt have amused him no end. Behind this eccentricity though, Simon's interest in Poe was genuine and scholarly. Through the medium of the library's resources he had managed to acquire a Lea and Blanchard first edition from 1840 of *Tales of the Grotesque and Arabesque* in two volumes. Only 750 sets were ever published and consequently have become something of a Holy Grail for all well-heeled collectors.

Poe's inscrutable face stared down at me with just the hint of repressed intensity. After a while, this scrutiny began to make me feel uncomfortable, the prospect of vivisepulture, black cats and subterranean torture chambers flooded into my consciousness. As an antidote to such horrors I tried to concentrate on the many conversations I'd had with Simon about the great man's work. Often these turned to Poe's invention of the detective story and the notion of ratiocination adopted by his detective Auguste Dupin. Shortly before his death I remember Simon outlining how the process of logical reasoning had been what had attracted him to the stories in the first place:

'The process of observation and inference from facts is a useful lesson in how to conduct oneself in life. That way one's opinions are invariably taken more seriously.'

I had made a rather feeble response to this pompous outburst.

'But surely Poe, by his own admission, abandoned the detective story after just three attempts because he saw the impossibility of an existence based only on logic. What of intuition, volatility and all the other human attributes that make us such complex beings?' I asked.

His response puzzled me to some extent.

'Ah, yes you have a point perhaps, but one should always try to confront a problem with as much logic as one can muster, at least as a starting point. We can all aspire to that can't we?'

'Yes, of course,' I replied, 'clearly there is an innate desire in all of us to act in a *logical* way, if for no other reason than to gain the respect of others.'

'Besides, I think you are being a trifle hard on Poe. There is a famous acknowledgement in his work of the need to balance logic with more, let us say, human impulses. I refer, of course, to 'The Purloined Letter', where, amidst the great logician's detective stories, we have an example of how logic and intuition, as you put it, combine in the most sublime way. Dupin himself indicates that by placing the hidden letter of the title in plain sight, amongst other documents in a place you would *expect* it to be, the Minister plays an elegant trick on his pursuers.'

'Yes,' said I, 'the distinction he makes is that the Minister is both a mathematician, endowed with all the logic that implies and, crucially a poet, too, whose creative force leads to his *coup de théâtre*. The point Poe makes is that Dupin must also understand the Minister's mind and possess the same qualities as him in order to unravel the mystery.'

As I stopped speaking a curious smile came across his

face as if he were remembering something that both amused him and flattered his ego at the same time.

As I sat there Simon's words filled my head and then seemed to swirl around the room, such that I was reduced to a trancelike state by returning Poe's hypnotic gaze. But after a while, an idea began to suggest itself. Where this came from I don't know, but something took control of me, guided my thoughts and brought enlightenment. I looked hard into Poe's staring eyes and then down at the *escritoire*, back to the portrait and again at the Sun King's present. This time my gaze was fixed. Without hesitation I got up from my chair and went over to the *escritoire*. There was a key in the lock of the drawer. I thought how odd in a piece so decorative to have left the key on show. I took hold of the key; it had merely been placed in the lock to make it look part of the piece – in plain sight. I took it back to the 'working' desk, it was a perfect fit. For the first time since Simon had died, I laughed. I should have seen through his subterfuge from the word go, but I applauded it, nonetheless, as an elegant conceit. At that moment I relived my dead friend's words and Poe's design: comprehending the psyche of an individual is the key to unravelling any mystery.

The drawer opened with a satisfying glide, but the contents were something of an anticlimax. Revealed was a manilla file clearly containing several papers and a large envelope which I retrieved carefully and placed on the desk. The file was bound by pink ribbon of the sort which is often reserved for legal papers, tied in an elaborate bow. Attached to the outside of the file by means of a rather rusty paper clip, was a letter. I paused for some reason, reluctant to intrude into someone's affairs, but Em had given me *carte blanche* to proceed and use my discretion. My first thought was that here were some legal documents which I could pass on swiftly to the family lawyers.

How wrong I was.

I undid the ribbon carefully and opened the file. A single photocopied sheet of what appeared to be sixteenth century script lay within. Before I examined it, I turned back to the letter on the outside of the folder. It was addressed to Simon from his father and I was astounded by the contents. I imagine the recipient was too. It was not long, and I reproduce it here in its entirety:

Dear Si,

I would normally wait for you to come down before burdening you with bumf, but the enclosed is of such importance to us all that I thought you should see it as soon as possible.

What I am sending you is a copy of a fragment unearthed recently amongst other papers written by Sir Simon de Betancourt from the 1540s. In view of the contents I am keeping a copy here under lock and key so please do not show it to or discuss with anyone. I have not shared the document with Em, and I think it best to keep it that way until we know more about what it means. To summarise, it seems that the rumour about hidden 'treasures' and the de Betancourts may be true and somewhere there are three 'devices' created by that wily old fox, Sir Simon, which are meant to resolve an ancient blight on the family. Unfortunately, only this small part of the key document survives, making the mystery even more elusive!

Anyway give me a ring when you have read them and perhaps you can arrange to come down for a weekend soon …
yours etc.

The mention of Sir Simon brought memories flooding back. It was his puzzle which had set off the chain of events which led to his namesake's death centuries later. Simon's description of his ancestor as we stood in the library during my fateful visit seemed strangely prophetic now:

"'Ah, the great Sir Simon, the house builder … He was a

formidable scholar and lover of puzzles and esoterica, and by all accounts a dabbler in the occult, although there is little hard evidence of the latter. There is a memorial to him in the local church … Quite a character!'"

I opened the file again and started to read Sir Simon's words:

It is of the gratest sorrowe and distresse to me that I must perforce rite such a melancholy legend, all the more so as it concerns my owne familee. My recent reserches in the Librarie have revealed to me the most shocking of truths, cruelle and wicked.

My story chronicles the dyre curse brought upon us the de Betancourts bye the most sinful of our cousins, Sir Richard of the most ill repute. When Ashcombe was an Abbeye most proper he did conspyre with the Abbot to commit the most foule of crimes against a noble Knighte Sir Edwarde Cavendishe. I have discovered the diary of the monk Odo and read of this deede therein. This murder and robbery bringeth shame to our line but know ye that worse follows. A book existed in this librarie, a historie of the evil Sir Richard chronicled secretely bye I knowe not whom. Even though he be my forbeare and I alas of his bloode, I herebye renounce him before God. I have this day destroyed this most loathsome document, so its very presence be not a temptation for further transgressions.

From this book of woe have I extracted the three outrages of Richard. I have lernt that before even the murder of the innocent Cavendishe Richard's name was notorious but of most infamous repute is his worship of the Infernal one and in the pursuit of this a violation of a most holy relique of our church. Then not even satisfied with this outrage and the death of the most respected Knighte he proceeded to exploite and defame yet two further of the most revered objects of christendom, for veneration of the Prince of Darknesse. This blasphemye hath set a curse upon the de Betancourt line whereby from divers times the evil will manifeste itself without favoure through the ages until an innocente will destroy such burthen. This prophesie hath I dremt. So as to hide such truth from malevolent eyes keene to thwart my intention I have with my own acumen and cunning constructed three explanations for the generations that followeth me. These trials are hidden from open sight, he who searcheth for them will do so in vaine. Rather they will become apparent in the naturel way to whomsoever would them decyphere. For my owne part I am unable to pursue this exorcism on my own parte for I am olde, sicke in body and watched by those of my loins who have succumbed to evil. Thus is the legacye of the accursed Richard.

He who resolves these challenges must return these most precious artefacts to their rightfule protectors. Only then will the malaise be gone. But let care be thy watchword at every turne the armyes of the nighte are against thee. The daynger to be faced is grayte and life will be at extreeme peril, if not forefeit.

At this point the strange document ended. The date on the letter was a year before Simon's much-loved father died, so it seems the document had languished in the desk for many years. Through all this time Simon had retreated into himself, initially out of a deep sense of loss and latterly out of habit. It had only been his marriage to Genie which had revived his spirits, only to be broken again by the tragedy of her death.

The consequence of this manuscript could not be ignored: there were *three* riddles set by Simon's namesake and undoubtedly the hidden paper in Brother Odo's book, found in the library, was one of these. For a moment, a sharp pang of resentment coursed through my body, when I thought of how this had been kept from me. But perhaps it was the manner of his death and the closeness of our friendship that would not allow me to condemn him outright. I still clung to the belief that Simon's behaviour had somehow been a form of temporary aberration and that keeping Sir Simon's document a secret was a sensible precaution against the possibility that the whole thing was a fake. But deep down there was a part of me too that recognised my naivety.

One thing was certain however, in the light of this discovery and the traumatic events of the night of Simon's death, the time had come to tell Em the whole story; too much had been kept from her. I would do so straight away. But even as I made this resolution one thought would not leave me, it made me quail to even think about it. The ominous words of Sir Simon began to haunt me ... the 'innocente', what if I ... ?

I

Oxford – two years later

It was not just the fact that he was dead, although that was shocking enough. There was something else. Perhaps it was the contorted shape of his face, the sunken cheeks, the deathly pallor, the spectacle of someone caught in the pose of death but yet carrying a memory of life. Or, perhaps it was the plight of a once great man reduced in death to a lifeless husk, the uncanny sight of a corpse occupying the chair from which so much vitality had flowed. None of these. It was the eyes; the wide, staring, panic-stricken eyes. What the rest of Henry Horatio Strickland's face merely suggested, the eyes betrayed. In the fathomless depths of this deadly gaze was an imprecation, as if the eyes were continuing, long after life was extinct, to warn of some incalculable evil. As I stood there transfixed by the horror before me a bizarre unspoken exchange ensued. There was no hiding from the lifeless scrutiny; like a bitter parody of the Mona Lisa his eyes were steadfast, enigmatic, and most chilling of all, unblinking. I had the overwhelming, terrifying impression that something had scared this most stoic of individuals to death.

A day that started ordinarily enough had suddenly become a nightmare, one which drew me into a centuries old Manichean conflict which lay at the heart of belief. My unfortunate discovery was the result of a whim, as I had not seen Strickland, or HH as he was known to his colleagues, for some days. Now, when I think of it, as I climbed the staircase for no good reason I sensed a strange unease; an echo, nothing more. When I arrived at his rooms I entered straightaway after knocking as, in that quaint Oxford tradition, his door was ajar and not 'sported', indicating that he was open to visitors. But instead of stimulating conversation, I was standing before the silent body of one of the University's most redoubtable figures.

Oxford has had many legendary teachers and men of letters over the centuries, but HH must surely rank amongst the forefront, even in this august company. In the field of Medieval History, he was a nonpareil, sweeping all before him in a cascade of literary awards and honours. His many books frequently became the definitive word on a given subject but all this approbation brought with it the resentment of his peers. In a place like Oxford where intellectual capacity is matched only by the size of one's ego, envy soon creates a climate of hostility. As such, HH earned respect, fear even, but never love, and dons generally avoided his company rather than submit, as they saw it, to his insufferable arrogance. Although junior fellows, as I was then, were generally pond life, and well down the food chain as far as HH was concerned, somehow he and I managed a *rapport* that was mystifying to others and, most of all, incomprehensible to me.

It was now two years since my experience at Ashcombe, during which time Em and I had married. Although we were living in Oxford she had retained her position with a large publishing house in London and despite the fact that this meant considerable travel and demanding hours, Em could not have been happier. She had long since come to terms with the strange behaviour of Simon at the time of his death and her exclusion from the secrets surrounding Sir Simon's document. As for me, I found University life idyllic and I soon settled into the rhythm of the days. At last, it seemed, our lives had regained some semblance of order.

Apart from our academic preoccupation, HH and I shared two abiding interests: the music of Bach which was almost an obsession with him and an interest in esoterica and puzzles of all kinds. We enjoyed a common indulgence as crossword setters, he as the renowned Aristoxenus, so named after the Greek philosopher of the Peripatetic School founded by Aristotle. His puzzles were notoriously difficult and many a solver the world over had reason to dread his particular sobriquet. In normal circumstances he was to others the model of inscrutability where his puzzles were concerned, but in the brief time I had known him, he had passed on many secrets of the art, rather as a prophet would to a willing acolyte.

But now I stood in disbelief, trying to take in the enormity of what had happened, most of all the proximity of his death. The same discomfort I had experienced on the stair had pursued me through the door. Its unseen presence pervaded every corner of the scholar's rooms to the extent that, had I possessed any religious convictions, I would have said that only an exorcism could rid the place of whatever it was that lingered there. It slowly dawned on me that he must have died a short time before I arrived. It was mid-morning and undoubtedly his scout would have visited him first thing in case there was some errand that needed running. Fellows of HH's standing were treated as royalty by the staff and invariably inspired a dog-like devotion from them.

This inertia passed and practical considerations took over. Authorities were summoned, people informed, and the sordid processes, inevitable in the wake of sudden death, took over. But even as I retreated from the scene I could not forget the cold stare of those eyes. For many nights afterwards and throughout the whole of the affair they followed me, fixated, disembodied, ineffable.

The circumstances of HH's death would give rise to much speculation in College; not even Oxford is immune from irrational gossip. During recent months he had not sought the company of his fellows and, apart from dining in Halls, little had been seen of him. Rumours abounded, as they often do in such a cloistered environment. Some said, no doubt as a kind of wish fulfilment, that he had begun to lose his intellectual powers and shied away from company, others that he seemed distracted by some important and secret enterprise. In the ensuing days news filtered through that the cause of death was a seizure brought on by high excitement or acute anxiety, no one could be sure which. Given that he had been, hitherto, a healthy individual there was inevitable speculation from those who believed that he was engaged in clandestine research, that this was the real cause of his death.

The funeral was held at Oxford Cathedral, in the city where he had spent the last forty years of his life. The congregation was very large; despite HH's peppery reputation, few doubted that they were witnessing the passing of one the most distinguished scholars of our age. Not only were the great and good of the University there to bear witness, but also many other luminaries from the media, politics and the arts. The wake was held in College, hosted by the Master, and it was here, for the first time, I met his elder brother, Christopher. I had heard something of him from HH himself, although very little of this was enlightening, except that he had spent much of his time abroad and now lived in the West Country. He greeted me warmly:

'Ah, so you are Jack Tregarden! My wife will be so sorry to miss you, struck down by 'flu I'm afraid. Harry (clearly the name used by the family) spoke of you warmly, not something he did lightly.' ·

'I'm very flattered', I said.

'Don't be, my brother never flattered anyone in his whole life. If he said it, he meant it.'

'I can assure you the feeling was mutual.' I replied.

'I gather that you had the misfortune to discover poor

Harry, that must have been an awful shock.' He seemed genuinely solicitous on my behalf.

I made no mention of the sinister circumstances I had encountered but merely expressed my sorrow at his death.

Inevitably our conversation gave me an opportunity to draw comparisons with his late sibling. Although at sixty-four, some six years older than HH, his whole demeanour was more robust. Like his brother he was well over six foot tall, but much more heavily built and it crossed my mind that I would not have cared to face him in a boxing ring. His handsome face, with chiselled features and enquiring eyes, belied his age; only his greying hair betrayed him. In all other respects he had held back the onset of the years with the confident and engaging mannerisms of a man half his age. This outward appearance conveyed someone at ease with the world, who had moved in elevated company. And yet, there was, I thought, some latent anxiety in those sparkling eyes, a barely hidden shadow which now haunted him.

'It is of some comfort to know that he had a friendship in College, I'm only too aware that he was not an easy man. I was used to his ways; because he didn't suffer those whom he thought to be fools if he did befriend you could never have a truer companion.'

I nodded. Christopher had been a senior diplomat for most of his life, so his frequent tours of duty abroad meant that contact with HH had been sporadic, although he did say that since his retirement they had seen much more of each other. Despite this separation from HH there was no doubt Christopher had his measure. I detected a genuine affection for his late brother in the way he spoke of him, almost sorrow, I thought. There followed a somewhat awkward silence before he tried to lighten the mood.

'One thing, I never could understand his bloody cross-words! I always thought I was a dab hand at them, but I must admit they had me struggling most of the time. But I gather you are not only an aficionado but a setter yourself.'

'I am not in his league although he did pass on a few tricks of the trade. But I agree with you his puzzles were amongst the hardest I have ever seen. To complete one gave me a real sense of achievement.'

'I'm sure you are being modest. I expect you know that some editors, even those of the most august outlets, used to complain that his puzzles were too difficult and that only a handful of solvers could complete them. You can imagine how that went down – 'bloody philistines' was one of his most frequent invectives.'

I smiled; these rants were very familiar to me.

'I think he found it hard to understand that there were some people just not on his wavelength and would never aspire to it.' I said.

Just then Em joined us and I introduced her to Christopher. This seemed to prompt a particular reaction: he studied her carefully, not in a lascivious way, but as if he had met someone who was important to him. After the usual niceties her presence seemed to awaken a particular train of thought within him as he quite suddenly changed the subject:

'I wonder … did my brother mention his most recent research to you, at all?'

His tone had become notably more hesitant as if the matter were delicate. There was a hunted look in his eyes and the confident man of the world I met a few moments ago had all but vanished.

'No, I don't believe he did', I replied, unsure of where this was leading.

He glanced earnestly at us both, seeming anxious to summon the means to say something of great importance, but his courage failing him.

'Oh, no matter then … I'm sure it'll keep.' He appeared to be talking to himself as much as us.

This proved to be a rather enigmatic ending to our conversation. The Master whisked him away to meet other mourners from the College but, as he followed, Christopher turned and gave us both a last, concentrated look.

Later as Em and I made ready to leave, she turned to me and said:

'Did you notice the way Christopher looked at us, both during our conversation and when he left with the Master? … And why did he ask about HH's research? I think he was dying to say something but held back for some reason. Are you sure you don't know what HH was involved with?

'Yes, absolutely sure. As you know I hadn't seen him for some weeks and he always was a secretive old so-and-so, so it's likely he wouldn't have told me anyway. There has been a lot of College gossip about it though since he died.'

'We've not the last you have seen of Christopher, I'm sure; I got the overpowering impression of unfinished business.'

The day after the funeral I sat in my room in college, trying to look forward to a term set aside for research into the literary codes and secret writing of the late medieval and renaissance periods, without the daily rigours of teaching. But through the mists of ciphers and codes I found myself returning constantly to the sight of HH in death. Still those eyes haunted me; there was something about that stare I had not comprehended. It had been worrying me since I first discovered the body that, even in death, HH had been desperately trying to convey some sort of message. What were those eyes saying that simultaneously gazed at me and past me in the same instant. It was like a still photograph forever displayed in my head, a moment frozen in time, a *mise en scène* constructed for the purpose of conveying a specific meaning. But how to read it?

A knock on the door jolted me out of my meditation. It was Baverstock, a senior don with rooms on the floor below mine. I must admit my heart sank when I saw him, he was a longwinded, self-important soul who only visited when he wanted to offload some unwanted task. My suspicions proved correct.

'Ah, Tregarden', he began, 'I have a job for you!'

Mindful of my junior status and future career prospects, and aware of Baverstock's close friendship with the Master, I put on the best face I could muster to hear the impending imposition. There were times when deference, however distasteful, had to be deployed:

'Yes Martin, what can I do for you?' I said, amazed at my sincerity.

At this encouraging response he beamed, his bald head shining in the reflected light. His beady eyes, set deep in his round face, surveyed me briefly for any signs of reluctance. Despite his habitual bluster, behind the mask was a rapier sharp mind capable of detecting the slightest demur and for a moment, I thought his cursory glance had seen through my pretence, but no, seemingly satisfied, he proceeded to unburden himself.

'It's Strickland', he said rather ominously. 'I need you to go through his room, more particularly his current work.'

The sound of HH's name had awoken my interest.

'But surely his effects have been taken away by his family?' I said, slightly bemused by the request.

'Well, the scouts will remove most of it. His only close relative was his brother and he just wanted a few personal items, but he has asked that someone go through the books and academic papers before deciding what to do with them. HH owned a house in Oxford, as you know, but that was let on a long lease a few years back, so that is taken care of. Really what's needed is for someone to go over what remains. When I say "someone" Christopher Strickland asked for you specifically.'

I expressed astonishment that someone of my junior status should be entrusted with such a prestigious task.

'Well, I must admit to some surprise myself. Both the Master and I hesitated, but considering the generous bequest left by HH to the College, with Christopher as the executor we felt … ahem … that we should accede to the request.

My initial thought was, thank you, but not very much for your unerring confidence in me, you pompous buffoon. Tact, of course, prevented me from saying anything. Leaving aside the condescension, I too was genuinely taken aback by this sudden invitation. My thoughts turned to Em's comments after the funeral, just how much did Christopher know about me and why was it so essential that I should be the one to review his brother's last work? My head became clouded with doubt, filled by questions without answers. I managed only an inadequate response:

'Christopher asked for me you say? That amazes me. We're both medievalists certainly, and like me, he was fascinated by esoterica and symbols, but surely a more senior Fellow …'

'Oh, come now Tregarden, why so coy, everyone in College knows you were his blue-eyed boy.' There was a bitter edge to his voice. 'He was a funny chap I'll give you that (Oxford code for "none of us liked him, and the feeling was reciprocated") but this is your opportunity to review, catalogue and collate the work of one of our greatest scholars. Surely you wouldn't want to pass that up, would you?'

He had the uncanny knack of making an opportunity seem like a thinly veiled threat. In this particular case, however, no threat was necessary:

'It'll be a pleasure; I'd be honoured to do it.'

He gave me one final look of disdain, nodded and left. My relief at his departure was tempered by the turn of events. I could not escape the thought that the request had really come from HH himself, his brother being merely the intermediary. How else to explain my involvement, I was an unknown quantity as far as Christopher was concerned and whatever had passed between the two brothers while HH was alive, somehow an understanding had been reached that I was to be approached. This begged an unthinkable question: had HH expected to die? Surely this was too fanciful, what could it be about his work that made him fear for his life?

I realised that my mind was beginning to run away with me, there might be the most innocent of reasons to explain the request. Perhaps HH just felt close enough to me and happy enough with my work to trust that I would be faithful to whatever it was he was writing about. I could see that would be the sort of thing he might convey to his brother, considering the somewhat testy relationships he had in College. For a moment I convinced myself, but the image of his death reappeared, the face of a man in torment, and I felt only a creeping apprehension and an intense sorrow.

II

Baverstock's visit had left me rather disconcerted. To curate the last works of such a titan was a once in a lifetime opportunity for any scholar, let alone a junior fellow such as myself. I could see my term of research receding into the distance, but the more I thought about it, HH's interests and my own frequently coincided, so who knows what new insights it might give me. Slowly, I began to look forward to the future with a little more enthusiasm.

The truth was that HH had done very little teaching latterly and had assumed the role of a senior research fellow with assiduity. He was the kind of forbidding academic who made Masters or even Vice-Chancellors quail, his boorish ways tolerated by the University solely on account of the quality of his scholarship. In recent years he had written a number of highly original works on the medieval and renaissance period which had never failed to astound and provoke the wider academic community by their sheer originality. His work on the Wars of the Roses, for instance, shed a completely new light on the hitherto unknown but pivotal role in the conflict played by certain foreign royalty, thus changing much of the received wisdom on the period. This brilliance was, however, in sharp contrast to the lack of what are now referred to euphemistically, as social skills. Once, the University made the grave error of allowing him to appear on television in a live discussion with other historians in which he proceeded to demolish their books and opinions to such an extent that the chairman of the forum had to bring the 'discussion' to an early conclusion.

I decided to carry out a preliminary survey of his papers to gauge the size of the task in front of me. It meant a return to HH's rooms.

I had climbed the staircase to Strickland's lair on many occasions but not since my grim discovery of the previous week. To do so now felt uncomfortable. The vestiges of that fatal visit clung to me like an incurable distemper, stifling any attempt to break free. Tentatively, I turned the key in the lock and opened the door to the rooms. The curtains were drawn and in the fading light of an autumn afternoon the stagnant air hit me at once. Paradoxically, my reaction to this miasma was an icy shiver; all the tension which had built up inside me was released in an algid frenzy. In some perverse way, I had convinced myself that somewhere in these rooms lay the key to the mystery of HH's death.

Strickland's 'set' consisted of a spacious sitting room, a bathroom, study and bedroom. The sitting room typified the realm of an ascetic bachelor. No obvious effort had been made towards comfort; a small settee was set amid two aged leather armchairs, as if arbitrating some ancient dispute between them. A ring-marked coffee table stood sentinel in front of an empty fireplace and a couple of dining chairs paid casual attendance to the most attractive piece of furniture in the room: a dropleaf Pembroke table on which rested a rather ancient radio, a mass media interloper in an alien world. The atmosphere was one of overwhelming stillness and silence, as if waiting patiently to be resuscitated by the return of its august inhabitant. It soon became clear to me that nothing had been touched since the moment of his death. This abstraction had been taken so literally that it was hard to believe that HH had died at all. Newspapers lay where they had been set down, stray books which, having escaped their shelves, were stranded in unaccustomed places, a familiar tobacco pouch teetered precariously on the edge of a mantelpiece, various miscellanea had been discarded at random and, most chilling of all, a pair of abandoned glasses, which I had seen HH wear many times, seemed to regard my presence with deep suspicion. These traces of a former life lay like dead soldiers on a battlefield, abandoned, their purpose suspended in a space where it seemed time itself had ceased to have any function whatsoever.

Through a door leading off the sitting room was HH's study. It was a large square room lined chaotically with books, not only the shelves on the walls overflowed, but the floor, the desk in the centre of the room, and even the windowsill. The scouts had not dared to touch his working papers, apparently they had been under instructions not to move anything until I gave the go ahead. Treading carefully around the desk doing my best to avoid Goethe, Montaigne and Shakespeare, I fell into a chair and immediately recoiled in horror. Without thinking I had usurped the very seat where I had found his lifeless body. A pulse of mortality ran through my whole body; I was an intruder, guilty of some unforgiveable sacrilege and damned as a result. Several moments passed before I could collect myself, so self-conscious did I feel, and even then I could not concentrate on the contents of the desk itself. Instead my attention wandered idly to the many pictures which covered every wall.

Prints of the Rotunda, the Parthenon, the three Graces, Daedalus' great Cretan labyrinth and other classical scenes gazed down with timeless repose. But my eyes rested on a series of pictures that HH had treasured as much as any of his books. I recalled his obsession with idiosyncratic buildings of irregular shape and how he came alive when he described them. There were many in this extraordinary collection and they occupied virtually all the available wall space not taken up by shelves. They were in various mediums: watercolour, oil, pencil, pen and print and were the result of years of pursuit and serendipity. He was aware how much I admired them and during the course of the last couple of years, I had acquired an intimate knowledge of each and its provenance. I was pleased that these had not been removed by his brother as they seemed so at home in HH's study.

My head was filled with vivid memories of our friendship as I gazed again at the early print of Sir Thomas Tresham's 1590s' homage to the Holy Trinity, the Rushton Triangular Lodge, alongside the five famous Round Houses at Veryan in Cornwall, originally built by a missionary named Reverend Jeremiah Trist for his daughters. HH loved the quirkiness of a round house where there are no corners for the devil to hide in. I saw once again the extraordinary asymmetry of Barcaldine, one of the castles built by Black Duncan Campbell of Glenorchy. Less sinister, but equally eccentric, was the watercolour of A La Ronde, the amazing sixteen-sided house in Devon, a product of two sisters' Grand Tour. This miniature masterpiece, completed in 1796, was supposedly based on the Basilica of San Vitale. The more I looked, the more I was saddened to think that the man who had so lovingly put together these beautiful images, would never see them again.

The sight of these familiar scenes had such a calming effect on me that I felt able to make a start on the mass of papers which were piled up in front me. But just as I did so my attention was drawn to a picture, immediately opposite the desk, which I did not recognise. It was an ink drawing in a rather battered old wooden frame of what appeared to be a hexagonal stone building, which could easily have been of the same vintage as Tresham's, but somehow I *sensed* the presence of a greater antiquity. Where this feeling came from I have no idea, but nonetheless the conviction grew the more I examined it. From far back in time faint images of ancient silhouettes, now indistinct but present all the same, flickered into life. The vagueness of these sensations did not obscure my awareness of an overwhelming malevolence; something deeply troubling blighted this place.

Although I recoiled from the picture, I had to admit there was something powerful and compelling about it that demanded attention and so, inevitably, I began to study the drawing more closely. As far as I could make out, the building stood on a mound of indeterminate size; so much space was taken up by its presence that there was little room for the depiction of the surrounding landscape. The dark stonework glowered back at me, subverting what could have been an aesthetically pleasing geometric shape, so much so that the building took the form of an alien malignant growth lately sprung from the earth. The artist, too, had managed somehow to enhance the sense of mystery by shrouding the structure in a mist that gave the impression of a building emerging from a primordial past. Undoubtedly, this was HH's latest addition to his collection, which must have been acquired during the last month or so since the last time I had visited him.

The longer I sat at the desk, the greater was my sense of disquiet. I was aware of lapsing into a kind of stupor where the distinction between reality and imagination became irrevocably blurred. Then it began. At first it was no more than an eerie sensation, but gradually my head was filled with a ringing sound. It was not the melodious peal from a church tower, but more like the relentless, resonant tolling of a passing bell. Such was the effect that I put my hands to my ears in desperation. But still it persisted. Then, without any warning, a figure appeared in front of the building; across a void of time and space we stared at each other as if transfixed, despite the impossible divide between us. The features were indistinct, but this did nothing to disguise the sense of evil emanating from his presence. I felt helpless in the grip of this strange fascination, feeling that I could only turn away when it was ready to release me. Eventually I came to my senses, to find that the figure had disappeared, and the ringing gone from my head. I was left with a real sense of terror, an exquisite, all-embracing terror. But instinctively, I knew that I had crossed a threshold into an unknown world and that this was a beginning, not an end; a relentless force had entered my being and would not be ignored.

The day had turned dull and overcast taking on a gloomy and oppressive aspect. Pale shadows filtered through the window and landed reluctantly on the paper-strewn desk; I wondered what, if anything, I could make of it all. The first task undoubtedly, would be to collect all the material and try to catalogue it before examining the contents in any detail. I decided that the best thing to do would be to retrieve what files I could from his side table, pile up the loose papers and take them back to my rooms. Then, once I was sure that all the relevant documents were in my possession, the scouts could pack up the books and other effects.

Just as I was finishing I heard a sound from the sitting room. For a moment, I froze. To my relief, a familiar face appeared round the door to the study. It was Priestfield, HH's long standing (and long suffering) scout. He had been with the great scholar as long as most memories could serve and probably knew him better than anyone else. His short, dapper figure and balding head were one of the most familiar sights in the College precincts. His face bore its familiar eager-to-please look cultivated over a long period of servitude. He always gave the impression that he was busy and you felt that if no work was immediately to hand, he would soon find some. He was his usual cheery self:

'Hello sir, I thought it might be you. Goodness, you look pale, are you quite alright?' He asked.

'Ah no, just seen a ghost', I replied. The subtlety was lost on him and he smiled awkwardly. He continued with his irrepressible *bonhomie*:

'I know just the thing; I'll make you a cup of tea; that'll buck you up.'

His suggestion found no resistance from me and he made straight for the kitchenette area full of purpose. He soon returned with a tray full of steaming tea and some biscuits. There are times when to be around such unfailing optimism and affected deference can be tedious in the extreme, but then, in the shadow of a friend's death, the presence of Priestfield seemed like a blessing.

'You will miss Professor Strickland?' I prompted.

'Oh yes sir, of all the people I've looked after he was special. That said, he wasn't the easiest person to get along with. Many's the day he could be disagreeable, hardly talk to anyone. He didn't suffer fools y'see. But then you'll know that sir, you being his friend that is. When all's said and done it was just his way, I used to ignore him half the time and he'd soon come around. I think it must have been a burden to him being so clever 'n all, others just couldn't seem to keep up.'

I nodded in agreement, thinking that only a fool would underestimate Priestfield; beneath the obsequious exterior lay an astute intelligence. I was sure that somewhere there was a parallel universe where Priestfield was revered for his wisdom and boundless common sense. There was no doubt he had some interesting and perceptive views on his former charge and the more he spoke the more curious I became. After a moment's silence he began again.

'I hope you don't mind my saying, sir; he was very fond of you. Sparing your blushes, he always said that you will go a long way in this University. "First rate mind" was his favourite phrase where you were concerned. He seemed to enjoy his time with you in a way he could not with others. There I've said it. I hope you will forgive me for blabbing on and embarrassing you, but it's the truth all the same.'

I waved away his apology, but as I did his mood suddenly

darkened. I noticed that he was staring at the same picture which had so held my attention earlier. This seemed to awaken unhappy memories for him:

'You know he wasn't himself for the last few weeks. It was all the talk of the College as I expect you know. He had something on his mind, and he used to say that it was one of the most important things he had ever been involved with. It's amazing that he would share these things with me, an uneducated man, but he did.'

He paused.

'Tell me what he said, if you're able to that is', I prompted, intrigued.

He thought for a moment, then he said, 'I suppose it doesn't matter now he's gone, and I'm sure he'd have wanted you to know. I only heard fragments mind you, he wasn't in the mood to talk too much towards the end.'

'Thank you, I would love to hear about the last few weeks especially as I have been away and hardly seen him. It would help fill in some large gaps.'

He looked again at the picture.

'I think it all started with that.' He pointed to the wall. 'He bought it locally in an antique shop, I don't know which one, but from that moment he was a changed man. He would spend ages looking at it. Then one day, the week before he died it was, he'd been away somewhere, and I came up to his room and he seemed excited. It was the kind of excitement that comes with fear if you know what I mean. He was standing in front of that picture. "I was right!" He said, "I've seen it, touched it even, but the trouble is I may have disturbed ancient powers. One thing's undeniable, this is a discovery that will make people sit up and take notice. Quite remarkable really." But beneath all the bluster, sir, I could see he was worried. Since then he was like a man in dread for his life. He would ask me constantly whether I had seen anyone suspicious lurking about. I did my best to reassure him sir, honestly, I did, but he was like a man lost, if you know what I mean. If you want my opinion, I don't think he was truly happy from the moment he bought the wretched thing.'

'Do you have any idea where Professor Strickland went during his last absence?' I asked.

'No, I'm afraid I don't sir. He was away for four days so he had plenty of time to travel some distance. When I asked if he'd a good time he just came out with all that stuff about him being right and so on. I don't think he wanted to tell me to be honest. One thing I am sure of though, wherever it was he went he took that picture with him.'

There was an awkward silence, Priestfield was clearly emotional. I hadn't realised just how deep his affection was for HH. Instinctively, we both turned to the drawing again. It was hard to see why such an innocent-looking object should create such feelings; but it was interesting to hear that Priestfield's reaction was the same as mine. The shadows that had begun to creep across the dead scholar's rooms now enveloped us. We stood there in the crepuscular light, each slowly fading from the other's sight, isolated by the impending gloom. It seemed that only the picture retained any form of luminescence and even that had the anaemic pallor of death. Eventually Priestfield broke the silence by clearing away our cups, after which he left. I was glad he had come.

I remained there for some minutes scarcely able to reason, my eyes fixed on the drawing. Having baulked at it before, I was sitting once again in HH's chair at his desk.

Then, out of nowhere, an epiphany!

My mind returned to that ambiguous stare on the fateful day. I was now sitting in precisely the same place and at the same angle as HH had been when I discovered him. I rose out of the chair and took up the position where I had been standing when I found him. There was no doubt about it. In his direct line of sight would have been the picture, just to my right and behind me on the wall, little wonder he had appeared to be looking both at me and the mysterious drawing. It was probably the last thing he ever saw.

III

After the encounter with picture, I felt an overwhelming urge to withdraw to the sanctuary of familiar surroundings, so I scooped up what papers I could for the moment, intending to return at a later date, and left. Since the wedding Em and I had taken a small house owned by the College about half a mile away, but I had, of course, retained my rooms in the precincts for teaching purposes, and it was to there that I retreated.

Even here, a latent anxiety remained. I decided on a brief perusal of the documents I had brought back with me and was intrigued by the subjects which had occupied HH's final weeks. Cheek by jowl were papers on 'The Challenge to the Rise of Humanism in Renaissance Europe'; 'The Plantagenets and the Wars of the Roses: A Family Business'; 'King John, Saint or Sinner?' and many others in a similar vein. But these, mouthwatering as they appeared, were all within HH's usual historical aegis. What caught my eye were two series of notes, together with essay length papers, entitled 'The Legend of Tristan and Isolde' and 'Alfred, the Outlaw King'. Although his research and writing were often unorthodox, I had never known him to stray into these particular subjects in any depth. I had already formed an idea that all these last writings might make a book of essays, billed as his swansong, if I could manage to edit them successfully. Even better if I could present these final works as showing something of a new direction. It would be a lot of work, but I would consider it something of a pilgrimage.

At the bottom of the pile of papers I found a large enve-lope. Scrawled on it in HH's inimitable hand was 'Jack T' and at the top it was marked rather formally, 'Private and Confidential'. Rather unlike him I thought; usually when I received something from him it was on a scruffy piece of paper folded, not very neatly, in half. I couldn't think how I had missed it when I gathered things up, perhaps my desire to get away made me less observant. With renewed nervous energy, I tore it open and the contents spilled out on to the desk in front of me. In the time that I had known HH I had become accustomed to his eccentric ways and his delight in using me as a guinea pig for his baffling crosswords. But even by those standards what landed on my desk on that pale afternoon utterly amazed me. I found myself staring down at four rather shabby wooden spars and a small sheet of paper on which was written, in HH's familiar hand, the words 'Well Jack, what do you make of this?' These were the only contents of the envelope, no explanation or clue of any kind as to what they were or why he had sent them to me.

There was only one conclusion I could draw from all this: it was another of HH's little games he loved to play, this time even more abstruse than ever. I assumed that this was some puzzle he'd come across somewhere and thought I would be amused. No doubt he'd already solved it, whatever it was, and wanted to see how long it would take me to do the same. This piece of whimsey, however, came with a sense of the tragi-comic; I remembered with much affection the sheer delight he got from the obscure and the absurd but realising that this would be the last such diversion he would ever create. For the first time since his death I was near to tears; in the end it's the idiosyncrasies, which makes someone the individual they are, that you miss most of all.

Filled with this renewed sense of fondness, I was about to pick up the mysterious strips of wood again when the 'phone rang. It was Em to say that HH's solicitor had called, asking us to come and see him as soon as possible. Em sounded quite excited, but I could only wonder what on earth his solicitor would want with us. It must, I thought, be something to do with the papers left to the College, but why me, and even more surprising, why both of us? I vowed to return to HH's challenge as soon as time would allow.

The offices of Standwick and Martin soon dispelled any Dickensian preconceptions I might have had about stuffy solicitors' offices. They were modern, bright and bristling with apparent efficiency and purpose. We were shown in to see Mr Cartwright, a pleasant, almost to the point of blandness, middle-aged man who greeted us warmly. After the introductions, much to my surprise, he began with an abject apology.

'Please accept my sincerest regret that you were not informed about the terms of Professor Strickland's Will before. It was a gross oversight.' He said, seemingly relieved at having got that off his chest.

'But we have heard about the will, in fact I'm working on HH's papers at the moment.' I offered by way of mitigation.

'Oh no, Dr Tregarden, you misunderstand. I'm sorry, I'm not explaining myself very well. You see, apart from the College, both you and your wife are also legatees of the estate.'

We looked at each other in utter amazement.

'I'm not sure what to say Mr Cartwright. HH and I got on extraordinarily well but there was never any suggestion from him that he'd do such a thing and as for Em, she really did not know him that well at all. Ours was an academic association, a meeting of minds, if you like.'

Em broke in at this point.

'What exactly is the bequest Mr Cartwright?' She sounded exasperated at the lack of progress in the discussion.

'Forgive me before I tell you, I must impart some news that you may not be aware of, Mrs. Tregarden.' He looked at Em as if he were about to deliver the sermon on the mount.

Maintaining his gaze, what he said next astounded us both: 'you will not be aware, Mrs. Tregarden, but Professor Strickland was a distant relative of yours.' He held up his hand at this point as we both made as if to interrupt him, such was our surprise. 'Professor Strickland' he went on, 'was a de Betancourt, like yourself Mrs. Tregarden, through a common ancestor. His brother has all the information about that and will, no doubt, fill you in on the details at a later date.'

There was silence. The merest suggestion of old, unwelcome memories began to take hold, bringing with them shadows and fear. We both looked at each other lost for words, but it was Em who eventually asked the obvious question:

'Why on earth didn't he say so? I find it extraordinary that during all this time nothing, not a word, has been said to either of us.'

I could feel the tension rising in Em and, from nowhere, dark images of Ashcombe flashed across my mind.

I could see that Cartwright, too, was finding this whole business very uncomfortable. He was at least able to offer an explanation for HH's extraordinary behaviour:

'I have been Professor Strickland's solicitor for many years since my predecessor, the late Martin Seymour, died,' he added, 'and although he was an internationally recognised scholar, he was essentially a private man who made few friends outside his academic circle' (and not many inside it, I thought to myself). 'There were two reasons for his reticence. Pre-eminent was the desire to set his relationship with you, Dr Tregarden, on a footing based on friendship without any familial impediments.' Cartwright seemed particularly proud of this last phrase, so he paused, giving time for his guests to digest it fully, before continuing.

'Mostly, I think he was concerned about your reputation, that other colleagues might consider his association with you was merely a matter of kinship. I can assure you that it was not. I believe many of your colleagues set much store by a close attachment to so great a scholar, bathing in reflected glory, I guess. Jealousy has always been a powerful emotion, wouldn't you agree?'

We waved aside the rhetorical question, as clearly Cartwright had more to say.

'The other reason for his silence is rather delicate, but nonetheless I feel strongly that you are entitled to an explanation and I'm sure that Professor Strickland would have agreed. You see, he was acutely aware of the, how shall I put it, circumstances surrounding your traumatic experiences at Ashcombe and he did not want that unhappy affair to be an obstacle to friendship. Please forgive me for raising unwanted ghosts' (he will never know how accurate that statement was!) 'but there it is in a nutshell.'

He sat back with the air of someone who has rid himself of a great burden. Beads of sweat had formed on his face, the man looked all in.

Cartwright resumed his legal *persona* with some relish.

'To the business of the will. As you probably know, Professor Strickland did own a separate property in Oxford which is let, the reversionary interest and any income now passes to his brother and does not concern us today. The remainder of Professor Strickland's estate is in the form of liquid assets, bonds, shares etc., with some chattels and I'll come to those in a minute. Most of his considerable capital is bequeathed to the College for various projects but, in particular, for the inauguration of a new chair in Medieval Studies. I might say, as an aside, that he expressed the hope you might occupy it one day.' He paused expecting me to comment.

'That day, if it ever comes, is a long way off', I said.

He continued. 'Well, I thought I would mention it nevertheless. There is, however, a bequest to you, Mrs Tregarden, of some twenty thousand pounds free and unencumbered.'

I looked at Em. She remained passive; I think she was still

reeling from the revelation about Strickland's family connection to register the amount of her legacy (in those days it was a tidy sum).

'Turning to you Dr Tregarden,' Cartwright pressed on, 'Professor Strickland has left you the choice of any of his books, the remainder will pass to the College. In addition, my late client wishes you to have his collection of paintings, prints, and drawings of various buildings which hang in his rooms. I believe you are familiar with the pictures in question.'

A chilling irony, I thought.

'Oh, yes', I replied breezily, 'I have often admired them. It is most generous of HH to think of me in this way.'

'I believe the collection is worth a considerable sum.' He said.

'The value is inconsequential; I would never sell it.'

'Oh, quite I was just eh ...' He added hastily. 'Anyway, I think it would be prudent for you to remove them from the late Professor's rooms as soon as possible for safety's sake. I haven't as yet obtained probate, of course, but as the executor of the estate, I'm very happy for you to do so. Someone will be contacting you in due course, no doubt, for valuation purposes.'

But that was not quite all. Just as we were ready to go, there came a intriguing footnote.

'So you can expect Christopher Strickland to contact you soon, I'm sure you are eager to know about the family connections.'

Em gave me one of her knowing looks, that said 'I told you so'. I smiled back.

As we left the office, my head spun with the thought of wooden spars and strange summonings, of King Alfred and sudden death, but most of all I could not get the image of the mysterious building out of my mind ...

... In a strange dark structure on a distant hill ancient impulses were awakening.

IV

The events surrounding HH's death and the aftermath had come at an awkward time for us both. Em was due to fly to the States on publishing business for a couple of weeks and the news of her mysterious family connection with the Stricklands had been a distraction she could have done without. For my part the supposed research term was taking on a very different complexion, and while the prospect of editing HH's last work was mouthwatering there remained the troubling impression that my life was slipping out of my control.

I had arranged with Priestfield to transport the picture collection to our house, but Em had to leave for America before she could see them for the first time. As she left, I could sense that her mind was still focused on events here because she made me promise to let her know the moment I heard from Christopher Strickland. At least she was able to stay with friends in New York, rather than be alone in a soulless hotel room. I was glad too that, given everything else that was happening, I had not told her about the strange experience with the picture, for fear she would worry I was lapsing into old traumas. Perhaps by the time she returned the whole business would settle down, but somehow, in my heart of hearts, I knew that was a vain hope.

The next day Priestfield and I busied ourselves with the pictures, taking great care not to damage them. Priestfield, in his own inimitable way, wrapped each one meticulously in tissue paper, and packed them in crates for their short journey across the city, it seems he was just incapable of doing a job other than thoroughly. I sensed too it was a labour of love for him, seeing the collection go to a safe new home. There would undoubtedly be other memorials to HH, but this one was personal and so brought both of us closer to him again. For the first time I had an opportunity to have intimate contact with the whole collection; the more I handled and studied the pictures the more I realised what a generous gift it was. There were over thirty in all, which I laid out on every available flat surface I could find. Included were fine pieces by notable twentieth century artists such as Piper and Bawden, but also much older drawings too. But try as I might my attention was constantly drawn to the strange hexagonal building. Priestfield saw me gazing at the picture, I could feel that he was fighting back the urge to say something. Finally, he could resist no longer:

'If there's nothing else, sir, I'll say cheerio if I may. Just one thing, I know it's none of my business, but if I were you I would get rid of that thing.' He pointed to the picture. 'As I said before, it may have excited him, but I felt it was a kind of frenzy if you know what I mean. I know a happy man when I see one, and he wasn't …'

I thanked him for all his help and said I would give his advice serious thought. But even as I uttered these words I knew deep down that parting with HH's latest acquisition was an impossibility. I did not try to explain this to Priestfield for the very good reason that I was at a loss to understand it myself. An indefinable compulsion had taken control of me which demanded I get to the bottom of whatever it was that had so preoccupied HH about this drawing. I owed him that much.

After Priestfield left, I looked again at all the pictures and wondered where on earth I would put them all as our modest town house seemed to be a woefully inadequate place for display. It occurred to me that I might loan the collection, or at least part of it, to a gallery so that the public could have a chance to see it. I had no doubt that its quirky content would be popular. I thought too, that HH would have been rather pleased with the idea and proud to know that his singular obsession might become a focus of interest. I decided to wait until Em returned and discuss it with her, after all she had not even seen the collection yet.

With a certain amount of trepidation I picked up the drawing and looked closely at the detail of the composition. My first reaction was relief that nothing untoward took place, and buoyed by this, I handled it with much more confidence. Now at last I had the opportunity to carry out more of a forensic examination to see whether I could discover some of its secrets. My initial disappointment as to its quality was not dispelled; despite the obvious power it possessed the picture itself was an ill-defined and outwardly unremarkable specimen. That in itself was a mystery: what was such a prosaic piece doing in HH's collection? Over the years he had become quite the connoisseur of this particular kind of art, and most, if not all of the collection, contained examples of excellent workmanship by artists of some repute. Even where the creator was little known or anonymous the quality was maintained. So I asked myself again, why? The only logical explanation I could give was that it was purchased purely for the subject itself, rather than any particular artistic merit.

I turned again to the focus of the strange picture. The building was clearly old but of indeterminate antiquity; from the drawing it was impossible to make any judgement about its location, save only that it appeared to rest on a nondescript hillock in an otherwise even landscape. The style and size of the structure was that of a folly, clearly built as an adornment for the knoll on which it stood. The architecture did not seem to be ecclesiastical, so it was probably safe to assume that this was the whim of a landowner. A trawl through reference books might yield an answer but I asked myself whether I could really spare the time on what may be a wild goose chase.

After all, if the building were well known I'm sure that HH would have acquired a grander depiction of it by now. No, this was a relatively obscure subject which for some reason possessed a personal interest for him, I was sure of it. What other reason could there be for his excitement over such a mundane work? Perhaps it was connected with the mysterious research of his last days which had encouraged such speculation in College. The triumphant, if frenzied, note he had struck, according to Priestfield, suggested a breakthrough. Interesting though these suppositions were, they were of no help for the purposes of identification and without this critical information I could make no progress at all.

It did briefly occur to me that I might ask whether any of my colleagues recognised the building but then I remembered that HH had deliberately kept the nature of this work secret. I suspect the last thing he would have wanted would be for me to go asking questions of others. Many knew of my involvement with HH's legacy and, would, no doubt would have connected the picture with HH and his research.

My hope was that the materials used in the construction of both the frame and the picture might reveal more. It was not large, some fifteen inches square, so hardly a grand piece by any imagination. The age of the drawing, however, was much harder to judge; the style could have been sixteenth or seventeenth century, but I was unsure. The frame was hardly prepossessing; a simple unpainted, worm-eaten wooden moulding rather the worse for wear.

With some trepidation I examined it more closely in the hope of finding a clue to the artist or a title, but to no avail. It occurred to me that sometimes on the back of paintings and prints someone has written either the location or at least some information which might help me. As I turned it over I could see that the mounting at the rear was new, or at least had been resealed recently. The joints were fresh and there were traces of an earlier repair clearly visible. This intrigued me. Had HH been struck by the same thought as mine? There was only one way to find out. I tugged at the surrounding tape and to my relief it came away; once this was free it was a simple task to ease out the drawing from the main body of the frame. My sense of anticipation rose as I removed the backing and coaxed the drawing from its mounting, such as it was. But disappointment followed. The drawing itself was made on a thick coarse parchment of cheap quality there being neither indication of the artist, nor any clue as to the whereabouts of the building. In fact, no mark of any kind was visible.

Perplexed by my failure to make any progress I replaced the drawing, mounting and backing as best I could. I surveyed the reassembled picture again, this time concentrating on the frame. Having been dismissive of its shabbiness earlier I began to revise my opinion somewhat. There was no doubt that it was careworn, but the joinery was of better quality than appeared at first sight, the corner joints being expertly mitred and the ornate folds in the wood created with much attention to detail. I judged the date of the frame to be contemporaneous with the drawing, perhaps sixteenth century and certainly of oak. Just as I was about to put it down in frustration I noticed that there was a recess in the frame which was a lighter colour than the rest of the wood. This groove went continuously right round the frame giving the impression that it had been subjected to less light, and therefore had not accumulated the grime and discolouration of the centuries. This strip was barely more than half an inch wide and the only explanation I could give for it was that it had been covered for most of its life and removed relatively recently. But it begged the question: what had been removed in order to create this effect, and why?

I had the answer to both questions in an instant. Without delay, I hurried back to my room at College alive with the prospect of discovery. There, lying on my desk where they had tumbled out of the envelope were the four strips of wood. I scooped them up without ceremony into the envelope and returned impatiently to our house. Once there it took me a matter of moments to confirm that these innocuous pieces of wood were in fact the missing beading from the frame of the picture. Not only were they the correct length and width but they were clearly oak of a similar colour and vintage to that of the main body of the frame. Flushed with pride at my discovery, I soon learnt that it was to be the easy part of this whole affair.

I considered the four wooden spars for the first time. Why were these so important to HH? On one side, the outer, the surface matched the moulding on the frame but otherwise there seemed to be nothing of note to see. The other side, at first sight, also appeared blank. Frustrated, in desperation I held it under the light and after straining my eyes for a minute or so, suddenly I saw it. Faint and worn with age were letters inscribed into the wood all along the length of each spar. I now realised that these four pieces had been fixed to the frame by means of an adhesive; my guess was some kind of an animal-based glue which became more widely available by the sixteenth century. This process had been undertaken with the utmost care; only the thinnest coat had been applied so that it had not obscured the lettering. Even then, this must have been a particularly special preparation for its time because the result gave a translucent effect. Nonetheless, the glue's presence had dulled the letters to the extent that it was easy to miss them altogether. The more I looked I could see what was obviously a recent light scarring here and there where someone, presumably HH, had chipped away dried glue which concealed what was beneath.

I studied the letters on the inside of the beading, they seemed to be in an arcane script compatible with sixteenth century form. The next problem was making sense of the writing and determining the order in which the beading was replaced. I decided that if I could fathom out where each strip should go, a conventional approach with the beginning of the letters starting at the top and running clockwise round the frame was the most likely. I would not know whether this was correct until I had discovered which strip went where. It is funny but you would think that with all the strips appearing identical this would be a very difficult task. It proved easier than I thought: a quick process of trial and error revealed the minute differences of how each fitted with the other and into their slot in the frame. After a few minutes I had the whole beading restored to its original place. Having accomplished this I was then able to remove the strips and lay them end to end in what I hoped would be in sequential order. The arrangement I had made seemed to be confirmed by the fact that the top strip commenced with a three 'word' phrase spaced apart from the rest that had the appearance of a title. So far I was encouraged; but this euphoria did not last long.

Although it took me some considerable time to make out all the letters, many were faint or distorted by the glue, I eventually produced a complete series. But the result made my heart sink: I could make no sense of the wording on each of the four pieces:

Ilon E'me Regnat

T em n onaels itu ohti waa, espotae ll ihtuoh tiw aeert dma orIecn ehmorf n ire. Ya waneht e rehrevero

flliw I yats. D'yarrae rof ebehtessorc oske emiwon edl oh tah

- wyeht llaekeesre venhc uot. Ti emoct ahw yamesle yl erae den raelotw erehtyad. Oss ihtym

egnyl ttesfoe ht ero cslaez rofllas, tah tenog erofeb foytle urcdevre swas Iey kr amllew ll ireveneid.

I was mesmerised by this apparently meaningless jumble of letters and not in the mood to delve into such complexities there and then. Instead, I lapsed into a kind of stupor, where the inexplicable events of the last few days merged into a meaningless confusion. I'm not sure how long I sat there but I no longer saw the drawing, only disjointed visions. A nagging thought started to grow in my mind; I had already convinced myself that HH had indeed inspected the document in precisely the same way. Wilder thoughts began to circulate around my head. Had HH's whole purpose really been an invitation to investigate his strange bequest? Had HH realised he was in danger, hence his comments to Priestfield that he had disturbed 'ancient powers'?

It was then that I was aware of an incipient fear and as the feeling grew I sensed the presence, from somewhere deep in time, of a compelling force, seemingly the embodiment of wickedness greater than any I had hitherto imagined. As I stared at the picture images began to appear, not in a co-ordinated way but rather in the manner of a fractured memory, where only partial recall is possible. These grew more and more disturbing; gruesome torture, executions and other unspeakable depravities, some too sickening to recount, were paraded before me, always played out with the ominous building as a backdrop. For several minutes I was a helpless witness to all the extremes that man was capable of, and while the barbarity itself was vile enough, the realisation that these were inflicted by my own kind filled me with both terror and disgust. One particular scene, particularly vivid, featured the barbarous execution of a prisoner who was dragged to the scaffold, then hanged, drawn and quartered. I tried in desperation to look away, anywhere but at the picture, but to avail, I was held in thrall by some unseen power.

Gradually the images subsided. Such was my hapless state that I felt nothing but relief when at last these dreadful tableaux ceased. For some time, I have no idea how long, I sat there, immobile, trying to empty my head of every vestige of what had gone before. Eventually I retreated to bed, half wondering whether the horrors I had seen were the product of a mind fatigued by my obsessive pursuit of the puzzle which HH had set. Little wonder that sleep escaped me; instead, I lay there in a state of agitated limbo. Before long came the ringing … again. So remorseless was it that my senses were utterly overcome. Instinctively, I got out of bed in a futile attempt to see if movement would help me escape the relentless echo. I found myself at the window. The full moon so commanded the night sky that it produced a listless, sham daylight which cast long shadows on the streets below. These imposters insinuated themselves into every corner of the scene. I was struck by the insidious way that darkness converts innocence into menace; so much so that the pleasant parkland opposite became, as I thought, a playground for myriads of demonic forces. The streetlamps were intended to relieve the gloom but instead their glow did nothing but exaggerate the corners of dense blackness. More than that, they produced an unnatural glare of the sort found only in the most unsettling dream. The effect was pure chiaroscuro: the eternal play of darkness and light, good and evil.

It was from one of these forbidden spaces that I first noticed the merest outline of a figure. It stood in the park next to the trunk of a large tree. So faint was the image in the dimness that I found myself doubting the evidence of my own eyes. All the time the remorseful ringing continued to toll. Then, as my eyes adjusted to such low levels of light, I looked in horror; there, in the shady recesses stood the figure from the picture. He, for it was clearly a man and of considerable size too, made no attempt to communicate, but just continued to stare upwards at my window. I could not make out any of the features of his face, save a deathly white pallor reflected from such light as penetrated the place where he stood. My mind, which had not recovered from earlier

47

terrors, was in turmoil. Eventually, I managed turn my head away, but no sooner had I had done so, than I was compelled to look again. In that instance of breaking the spell, he had gone and, just as before, so had the ringing. It was as if by the use of will power, which had seemed to desert me earlier during the evening, I had been able to rid myself of his presence. Exhausted, I closed the curtains and slumped back into bed, and lay there for the rest of the night in a hinterland between sleep and waking. The figure did not reappear.

In the morning, I awoke in a deeply distressed state; whatever it was that had entered my psyche I seemed powerless to exorcise it. Like Lear I was 'bound upon a wheel of fire'. It crossed my mind that if HH had indeed solved the mystery himself, he might have been through the same ordeal? If so, it was an alarming thought that, for him, it had ended in death. But there was little point in such speculation; only one practical step suggested itself: resolve the riddle in the hope that it would put to rest whatever it was that tormented me.

I finally abandoned any hope of the plans I had for my study leave and decided to devote what time I had to the problem that HH had set me. Elegant though it was, I found the antique script in which the inscription was written rather difficult to work with, so I copied the passage out as a continuous paragraph in my own hand:

Ilon E'me Regnat

T em n onaels itu ohti waa, espotae ll ihtuoh tiw aeert dma orIecn ehmorf n ire. Ya waneht e rehrevero flliw I yats. D'yarrate rof ebehtessorc oske emiwon edl oh tah - wyeht llaekeesre venhc uot. Ti emoct ahw yamesle yl erae den raelotw erehtyad. Oss ihtym egnyl ttesfoe ht ero cslaez rofllas, tah tenog erofeb foytle urcdevre swas Iey kr amllew ll ireveneid.

There did not seem to be any sort of pattern to it at all. I first imagined it to be some sort of cipher and so I applied all the rudimentary forms that I knew, such as A=1, B=2, C=3 etc., taking every other letter or every third letter and so on. I even tried starting from the back as well as the front. None of this worked. Having exhausted my knowledge of ciphers and codes, I began to lose heart.

I took out my frustration on the empty envelope in which the mysterious contents had arrived, snatching it up in anger. Just as I took aim with the intention of throwing it into the wastepaper basket, I noticed some exceedingly small handwritten lettering on the inside of the flap. In my haste the other day I had missed it completely. Despite my general state of annoyance I could not help but chuckle, it read:

Bach movement in poetic recital given by lesser German!

It was, of course, a crossword clue, perhaps the last one that this putative Aristoxenus would ever write. It occurred to me that only HH could augment a fiendish puzzle with yet another enigmatic idea. Despite this it was clear that if I could solve this it might cast some light on the main problem. At least I had the benefit of some insight into HH's clue-setting methods and the way in which his mind worked. Even so I toiled for a while before I began to recognise some of his tell-tale trademarks. The presence of the word '*recital*' indicated a homophone; putting this together with '*Bach movement*' I decided that the first two words constituted the definition part of the clue. Looking at the wordplay part, '*given by lesser German*' the verb '*given*' suggested a containment clue and after studying the phrase for a while I found '*regress*' set backwards in the two words, thus: '*le/**sser Ger**/man*'. It didn't take me long to relate this to '*Bach movement.*' HH used the word '*poetic*' to denote that favourite device of the Romantic poet in particular, the Imperfect Rhyme. In this context '*Bach*' relates to 'back', and so the wordplay, *'regress'*, is confirmed by the definition, *'back movement.'*

This discovery, however, left me slightly disappointed, because if regression was the key to solving the puzzle, I had already tried reversing the text without success. I looked at the wording again, more in hope than expectation, but I just could not see what it was that I was missing. Idly I played with the first part of the passage and tried again to overturn the writing and although I drew a blank to begin with, I did notice that a few words began to appear. Rather than using the existing configuration of nonsense words, if I reversed different groupings more words appeared. I cursed myself for being so stupid. All the time I had been misled by the existing sequence rather than working steadily across the page and reversing certain alternative formations, while keeping them in the same position. With this breakthrough, despite the incompleteness of the result, I felt sure I could make some sense of it eventually. The more I stared at it the more I could see words which were either joined on to others, or punctuation and spaces which were designed not to elucidate but obfuscate. Here my interests in crosswords came in handy. I decided the first thing to be done was to remove all of the existing spaces and convert the text into one long paragraph without any punctuation whatsoever. When I had done this I was able to see clearly all the proper words embedded in this continuous stream. After several hours of playing with the letters, I learnt that the trick was not to reverse a section, for instance:

T em n onaels itu ohti waa, espotae ll ihtuoh tiw aeert

which would become nonsense:

Treea wit houthi ll aatopse aaw itho uti sleano n met

… but to reverse groups of letters, apparent words, ignoring

all spacing and phoney punctuation. Thus the opening sequence of *T em n onaels I,* for example, if reversed would become *Met-on-an-isle.* As I continued further into the piece a sequence emerged:

Met-on-an-isle-without-a-sea-atop-a-hille-without-a-tree

Which in turn readily divided up into two recognisable phrases:

Met on an isle without a sea / atop a hille without a tree

One glance at these two phrases and it was obvious that they were a pair of rhyming couplets. What's more it seemed that it was the beginning of a riddle of some sort. Would the remainder continue in the same vein? Following my instinct, I began to set out the letters in verse form and to my delight after an hour or so juggling with the letters a series of three verses emerged, with an intriguing title:

Noli Me Tangere

Met on an isle without a sea
Atop a hille without a tree
Roam'd I hence from Erin away
Then here forever will I stay

Array'd before the crosse so meek
I now holde what they all seeke
Never touch it come what may
Else dearely learne to rew the day

So this my settlynge of the score
Zeal for all that's gone before
Of cruelty served was I
Ye mark well I'll never die

I sat back and studied the result. The original writing carved into the wooden beading was the work of a scholarly hand, there was little doubt about that. The flourishes of the capitals and the precision with which the letters were formed spoke of a skilled craftsman accustomed to producing documents of a high standard. So what on earth was someone of this calibre doing writing such doggerel? With some difficulty I dated the writing through its the style and spelling as characteristic of the sixteenth century and my experience of cataloguing libraries with books and documents of this age told me that both the writing and the drawing seemed to be of similar vintage. The parchment, frame, and drawing too, all appeared to be compatible with my estimate of the date.

This latter discovery gave rise to an interesting conclusion: if both the drawing and the frame were contemporaneous it follows that the picture's primary conception was as a puzzle or message rather than an artistic ornament. Certainly, that's how it looked, but to what end? And why? Clearly the deciphering posed as many questions as it answered, and much more work was needed before this mysterious bequest yielded its secrets.

The general structure and tenor of the verses, as far as I could see, fell broadly into the following categories:

1st verse – location
2nd verse – curse
3rd verse – revenge

The third verse clearly needed more information before I could understand it. The same principle applied to the 'curse', the question there being do not touch what? But the reference in the 'title' to the Bible, John 20.1. about the risen Christ was intriguing: Jesus appears to the Magdalen after the Resurrection to comfort her. At first she thinks he is a gardener but when she recognises him he tells her not to touch him – 'noli me tangere' (let no one touch me). Apart from indicating a possible ecclesiastical context, this information was of little use in identifying the building itself. So clearly, the first task was to divine the location; the rest would, hopefully, unfold naturally. Here my heart sank, as I found myself in precisely in the same position that I was when I first saw the picture in HH's room. I had no idea where this might be, certainly not from the drawing itself, anyway. The only thing I could do would be to analyse the text and see if I could solve its riddle. I was intrigued by the phrase '*an isle without a sea'*. This set my mind racing, could I think of such a place? Was this an island in a river such as the Thames eyots, or perhaps in a lake, even somewhere like Inchmurrin in Loch Lomond? But hard as I thought no inspiration came that would fulfil the requirements for such a strange building. I decided, in the spirit of Samuel Johnson, to allow the triumph of hope over experience and await enlightenment.

At least the succeeding lines were a little more straight-forward. They seemed to imply that this place was the site of a burial: perhaps the building was erected as some sort of monument to whoever lay there. The Irish connection was interesting. A thought flashed across my mind that this scene may, at its heart, concern something far older than at first glance. This idea would reinforce the curious impression I had of the drawing when I first saw it in HH's rooms. There seemed to be a tenuous ecclesiastical connection but, intriguingly, the reference did imply coercion of some kind opening up the possibility that this could be the grave of a notable recusant. All this was pure speculation, nothing tangible at all to build a solution on. For the time being I gave up.

Long after I put the puzzle aside a thought lingered, one which brought a shiver, that I was almost certainly engaged in the second of Sir Simon de Betancourt's 'mysteryes' …

V

In dreams that night I became trapped in an endless labyrinth of islands and curses, menacing buildings and treeless hilltops. But what most preoccupied me as I woke was the return of the anxiety which I had not experienced for two years.

All my instincts told me to distance myself from the affair while I had the chance. My mind returned to the equivocal feeling I had experienced when I first saw the picture. It is a funny thing about trauma and its latent effects: at its heart there is a fascination with that which we fear. As paradoxical as it may sound, I found this unconscious desire to be one of the most powerful elements of this whole ordeal. It was not something I could control. It is as if outwardly our instincts resist whatever phobia challenges us, but something at our core is unable to resist. Also, I felt an obligation; whether HH had intended it or not, I had been left with this puzzle and I felt the burden of trust on my shoulders. Whatever lay behind all this, it may have cost him his life and I couldn't ignore that. I saw too why he hadn't just written down the solution for me. Perhaps the secret was so dangerous that he didn't want it to be available for others to see. Yes, danger, palpable danger.

In this equivocal state I resumed the task of trying to interpret the rhyme, hampered by the fact that I dare not share it with anyone lest they be drawn in too. The more I looked at the wretched thing the further I seemed from a solution. After some hours I conceded defeat yet again and busied myself with more mundane tasks in the hope that a period of mental relaxation might just bring enlightenment. But none came.

Several days passed and I began to despair of ever making any progress. What's more I was missing Em very much, we had spoken a couple of times on the 'phone and I tried to sound cheerful on both occasions. I suspect she picked up my underlying anxiety. Quite apart from the joy of her everyday presence, she has the ability to think laterally, which without doubt would have led her to the answer. But her return was two weeks away. Having put aside my research project for the term, "Covert Writing in the Renaissance Period", I decided to rethink this idea, as a distraction for my clouded mind. To tell the truth, I half hoped that this subject, not unconnected with the problem left to me by HH, might help me. In a funny way it did.

One afternoon I was looking at the various devices used by spies and their royal patrons in the 1590s, when I came across the use of the acrostic as a common way of disguising messages. After all Sir Simon had used a loose version of it in the first puzzle concerning the library at Ashcombe. What if he had employed it again? For some reason a memory stirred … something I had seen in the three verses. Like an addict returning to his stash, I went back to the drawing and its enigmatic poem. But in a few moments my excitement drained away, I just could not recall what I thought I had seen earlier. The word acrostic had stimulated something, of that there was no doubt, but even with the poem in front of me … nothing came to mind. Just as I was trying to compose my thoughts the telephone rang, it was Baverstock. Martin bloody Baverstock! My heart sank, but fortunately he was, for him, fairly brief. All he wanted was to confirm some minor administrative point regarding College procedure and check on my progress with cataloguing HH's work. I did not tell him about the puzzle. I put the phone down with much relief and, suddenly, I remembered: 'Martin', or something similar, that was it! That was what I'd seen. I looked down at the verses in front of me and there it was:

Touch Me Not

<u>M</u>et on an isle without a sea
<u>A</u>top a hille without a tree
<u>R</u>oam'd I hence from Erin away
<u>T</u>hen here forever will I stay

<u>A</u>rray'd before the crosse so meek
<u>I</u> now holde what they all seeke
<u>N</u>ever touch it come what may
<u>E</u>lse dearely learne to rew the day

<u>S</u>o this my settlynge of the score
<u>Z</u>eal for all that's gone before
<u>O</u>f cruelty served was I
<u>Y</u>e mark well I'll never die

The first letters of each line spelt out MARTAINESZOY. I remembered now saying idly to myself, the first time I saw the poem, how the first few of these letters were MART, but I didn't take it further. Strange though the word was, it immediately gave me a clue as to the location. There was a place in England where the word 'zoy' was common – the Somerset Levels. I knew this from some research I had carried out into the Monmouth Rebellion and the Battle of Sedgemoor fought near WestonZOYland in 1685. If I had remembered correctly, 'zoy' was an old Somerset word for hill. So in all probability Martaineszoy was one such feature, which should not be too difficult to find. This revelation made it clear why HH was researching both the Tristan and

Isolde legend, with its Irish roots, and the story of Alfred the Great who hid from the Danes in the Somerset marshes.

I went to the library and searched the map of Somerset frantically. After scouring the area of The Levels I found Martaineszoy; it seemed to be a very small place judging by the entry. There was a church marked, and a quick piece of research elicited the name St. Martin's. Perhaps an anglicism of the Irish Martain, hence the reference in the acrostic. Was the connection with Ireland becoming clearer? I noticed too, that in addition to the conventional lettering for the village, there was a separate location marked **Martaineszoy**, in a style of lettering usually reserved for ancient sites. I wondered whether this was the mysterious building itself or perhaps the site on which it stood. It was then that I decided, come what may, I must go there.

When I returned home, a disturbing thing. I placed my notes on Martaineszoy on the table, went over to the picture and turned it so that the drawing was visible again. No sooner had I done this than I felt an icy draft fill the whole room and the ringing, which had begun to haunt me, welled up again. Shadows lengthened, and the light dimmed. A vague nausea took hold and I could barely summon the courage to look. Sure enough he was there. Bolder than before, he stood in front of the building, a sardonic, twisted smile on a cadaverous face. There was a devilry in this look that defied generations, eons even, immutable and soulless. It was an aspect as old as the world itself; the antithesis of all that was decent. As I gazed into that face I was convinced that what I saw was the eternal face of evil. With dread, I recited the final line of the poem to myself '…*Ye mark well I'll never die.*'

The longer I stared, dead eyes seemed to challenge my very existence. For one awful moment I thought he would walk out of the frame and come towards me, but instead his right arm rose slowly in a menacing gesture as if he were about to bestow an unholy benediction. The mouth moved in a ghastly, soundless mockery of mime. What he could possibly be saying was beyond me, other than something from the vault of the past that was far from desirable. When the silent peroration had finished, the figure vanished as quickly as it had appeared and with it the persistent ringing.

It took several hours before I felt warm again. The image, however, lingered far into the night.

As I was setting the picture down I was reminded of something I had noticed earlier in the day. Attached to the back was a small sticker with the wording 'Laurence Standish Art'. The name was very familiar to me as I had visited his shop in the city many times and got to know him reasonably well. He had been at the funeral, but our paths had not crossed that day. I made up my mind to call in tomorrow and see if he could shed any light on the provenance of the picture.

The next morning I found myself in the rather chic alleyway near the High where the gallery stood. Standish was a tall, elegant man in his sixties with a neat white beard and a fastidious manner, whose principal concession to member-ship of the artistic community was a collection of gaudy bow ties. That morning the colour was deepest red. I had not seen him in a while, but still he greeted me like a long-lost friend. Although his manner could be taken as unctuous, especially when dealing with prospective clients, underneath this apparent insincerity lay someone whose professional judgement was always to be trusted; the mere suggestion of selling someone a fake would have mortified him. After the pleasantries were over, however, he adopted a more sombre tone.

'I was so sorry to hear about Professor Strickland; over the years he has been one of my best customers. I never thought he was ill or anything like that, such a shock', he said with a forcefulness that rather took me by surprise.

'Yes, it's all terribly sad', I said.

There was a slightly awkward pause, before I took the picture out of its wrapping and laid it on the counter in front of him. The effect was startling. I have seldom seen such a sudden change in anyone. He blanched and for a few moments he seemed speechless, trapped in a vacuum between surprise and horror. Before I could speak, he said:

'So you have it now', was his rather enigmatic response. 'May I ask, did Professor Strickland give it to you, or …?'

'Yes, he left it to me,' I said.

'Oh, I see.' His voice was full of dread.

'I brought it along as I wanted to know a bit more about where it came from. Is there anything you could tell me about that?'

So preoccupied was he by the picture's reappearance that for a few moments it seemed he had not heard me. Then with an unsteady voice he said:

'It … it came from a house in the South West, I believe.'

'You *believe*?'

'Well, you know, it was a strange business. A few weeks ago I went to an auction in Somerset: it looked a very promising sale with a number of antique prints that I thought would attract some interest in Oxford. By the end of the day, I had managed to acquire eight excellent items of considerable interest. When I got back and unpacked, to my astonishment there were nine pictures! I needn't tell you which item was the extra one.'

He made a vague gesture towards the offending image which lay before us. Outside the wind rattled the door and fitful rain beat against the shop window; inside all was still as we looked at each other in silence. No words were necessary, we both knew the consequences of what he had said. After a while he seemed anxious to unburden himself of the full story.

'At first I thought that it must have been underneath one of my prints and I'd picked it up by accident. Needless to say

I contacted the auctioneers, whom I have known for many years, and told them what had happened. But they denied all knowledge of it, something they were able to confirm when they checked their records. The vast majority of the lots that day had come from country houses in the area, so they were able to check with some accuracy. After much to and froing they were certain that the picture had not passed through their hands. In short, they had no idea how it came to be there.

'By this time I was beginning to doubt my own sanity, something like this had never happened to me before. I felt in all conscience that I should offer the picture to the auction house as I was sure that it had come from there, but they were insistent that I should keep it.'

It was clear that the whole affair had troubled Standish a great deal. The evidence was written on his face and I could see that just relating the story was painful for him. Ambiguities such as this were alien to his ordered world.

He continued. 'That's not all. From the moment I had the picture in my possession a deep depression came over me and sales at the gallery dropped. My usual customers deserted me, almost as if they could not bear to come near the place. I know it seems fanciful to attribute such things to an inanimate object, but the coincidence cannot be ignored. It's an irresponsible thing for an art dealer to say but I wish now I had burnt the wretched thing. But it's not just that, as soon as I saw it I felt there was something wrong ... something, well ... unwholesome.'

The last word felt as though it had been wrung out of him. I decided not to tell him that I too had felt its power, he was in enough of a state as it was.

'I suppose you were glad then when Professor Strickland bought it.' I said.

'Oh, he didn't buy it, oh no – I gave it to him. Now I feel a twinge of guilt, I hope to God that it had nothing to do with his death. I swear to you that I did not force it on him, it was at his behest.'

'How so?' I said, intrigued by his last remark.

'Incredible really. He came to the gallery a couple of weeks after I had acquired it; he often called in, on the off chance I may have something of interest for him. You may have seen that charming watercolour of the Veryan Roundhouses he bought from me last year? Well, I had left the picture on top of a table here in the main gallery reception room and when he saw it his reaction was astonishing. He said "Good Heavens! I can't believe it! Where did you get this?" At least my conscience is clear, I told him the whole unvarnished truth. He listened attentively and to my amazement, he just said, "I'm not at all surprised, it was to be expected." You knew the Professor, Dr Tregarden, he was not a man to get excited, quite the reverse in fact, but I had never seen him in such a state the whole time I knew him. When I tried to find out what it was that he knew about the drawing, all he would say was that it might be the key to a lifelong search. Anyway, he asked me what the price was and the rest you know. I was glad to see the back of it and that's a fact.'

Not wishing to cause him more anxiety, I thanked him for being so frank and made to leave. I took up the picture, swathed it in its cover, just as I did so, Standish said:

'You will ... take care won't you?'

Back at the house I was still digesting what Standish had told me, when there came the expected 'phone call from Christopher Strickland:

'I believe that Cartwright has told you I would call. About Harry, I hope very much that you can spare some time to visit us soon. I have a story to tell you.'

'That sounds intriguing,' I said.

'I think you will find it so.'

I arranged to travel down to see them in three days' time,

when I would also be introduced to Patrick Monahan, just as Cartwright had indicated. Apparently, Monahan had been at the funeral itself, but had left to keep another appointment straight afterwards and so had been unable to attend the wake.

He had one last request. 'If I understand it correctly, you are in possession of a certain drawing.'

'Yes, that's right.'

'Please bring it with you.'

Before he rang off, I took down his address. It was this that made me gasp audibly, Magnaveney House, Canon*zoy*, in Somerset.

So Christopher lived in the very area indicated by the rhyme; suddenly my mind was alive with speculation.

I was perturbed, but not surprised, somewhat by the urgency which Christopher seemed to attach to my visit. It would be the first time for two years that I had ventured into the South West. During the intervening time before my departure, I maintained my determination to keep the picture out of sight, wrapped heavily in material, so that the days passed peacefully without further alarm.

VI

Nearly three weeks had passed since HH's death when I found myself driving to Somerset on a bleak, November day without knowing where events would lead. I found it incredible to think how much my perspective had changed towards the supernatural since my first encounter with the de Betancourt family. I recalled with some uneasiness the number of times in the past I had ridiculed others for their belief, citing the rationalism of scholarship as my watchword. Now, not only was I humbled by that arrogance but, since the episode at Ashcombe, I had acquired an acute sensitivity to the uncanny. Something which the picture of the strange building had clearly revived.

Despite my passing interest in the politics of the Monmouth Rebellion I had never visited the Levels before and the prospect intrigued me. I had decided to take an unconventional cross-country route, one reason being to visit Wells Cathedral and take in some lunch there. As I drove westwards it gave me the opportunity to muse on the purpose of Sir Simon's puzzles. Perhaps the simple truth was that as a cabbalist and necromancer he loved the idea of mystifying his successors beyond the grave. Was the discovery and restoration of three religious treasures really the object? If so, solving the first puzzle had not resulted in the recovery of the sacred book, and now there seemed to be the pursuit of another, as yet unidentified, artefact, if the verse found in the picture, *'I now holde what they all seeke'*, was anything to go by. I suppose what finally convinced me of an underlying imperative were the lengths to which Sir Simon had gone to conceal his riddles. Surely if they were mere exercises he would have made them more accessible? But so well hidden were they that the hiding places had lasted for centuries. No, the more I thought about it, *concealment was part of the plan,* but to what end I had no idea.

When I arrived at Wells I hoped to put these thoughts to the back of my mind and concentrate on the Cathedral Church of St Andrew the Apostle. This 'most poetic of the English Cathedrals' was the first to be built in the new Gothic style and its presence overwhelmed me. But even as I stood, enraptured by the amazing ingenuity of the four-teenth century 'scissor arches' and the translucent splendour of the Jesse Window, a shadow loomed over the scene. This spectre came in the form of a dark and malevolent structure which stood on a barren hill on a windswept plain. It was the antithesis of everything that I could see around me. It was hard to think of two more contrasting structures, not merely for their fabric but the purpose for which they were built. I mused on how the impulses and motivation of those conceiving these buildings is reflected in the character of the final construction. I am not at all a religious man, quite the reverse in many ways, but as I stood there amid such architectural wonder I rejoiced in a creation which attempted to celebrate the light of the world; whereas the Hexagon would seem to have been born purely out of darkness. As I thought about the consequences of this I was aware of the merest of shudders passing through my body as I left the Cathedral.

Rather than setting out straight away for my destination, I lingered in the Cathedral Close, to what purpose I could not say. Even as I hesitated my eyes were attracted by a bookshop in a narrow precinct nearby, proudly advertising itself as the venue for all local literature. It set me wondering whether I might find a book on the Levels which featured the hexagon building. So far I had been unable to find anything useful on the subject, which for such a singular structure I found strange. Perhaps I had been looking in the wrong place.

I entered the shop, which had only a few browsing customers presided over by an amiable host who acknowledged me graciously as I came through the door. If someone had blindfolded me it would have made little difference as the aura was unmistakeable. There is something unique about the smell and the atmosphere which suffuses a second-hand bookshop. It applies as well to the people who frequent them; lost to the world they scour the shelves with an air of hopeful languidness. The faint mustiness seems to foster an unhurried approach to life; however frantic life becomes outside, crossing the threshold into this world is to reach an oasis of calm. It had been a while since I had been amongst books and it felt good.

The bookseller noticed my equivocation and offered his assistance.

'Is there anything I can help you with?' He asked genially.

I hesitated for a moment, conscious of the cloak of secrecy which HH had thrown around the Martaineszoy affair. I decided, on reflection, that an innocent question about a book would hardly be considered a breach of trust.

'Have you anything on the vernacular buildings of the Levels, specifically in the area around Martaineszoy? There is very little in Pevsner.' I asked.

Did I detect the merest trace of anxiety on his face? If so, it was only for a moment and the friendly mask was soon restored.

'Well I only know of two buildings of interest there: the Church, which is Saxon in origin and very fine, and the … er … Hexagon.'

It was the first time I had heard the building being given a formal title and it came as quite a jolt. The way he had said the word, with heavy emphasis, implied darkness. For a few moments he was deep in thought, then he moved over to a set of shelves towards the back of the shop and scanned the contents carefully. Tentatively, he reached out and pulled down a couple of volumes and handed them to me.

'These might interest you, take your time to browse them there may be some others too but I've so many books it's difficult to keep track without referring to my catalogue.'

He ushered me into an alcove with a table and chair, I set the volumes down and began to inspect them. One was rather a glossy affair with many attractive photographs but only rather superficial text. At least it did have a picture of St. Martin's Church and very photogenic it looked; whatever else transpired I made a mental note to spend some time exploring its treasures. I must admit to being not too hopeful about the other book, it was a rather shabby affair and had all the appearance of an Edwardian edition. The title, however, was, if a little melodramatic, intriguing: *Mysteries of the Levels* written by a Septimus Black MA (Oxon.), FRS. Much as I had suspected from the cover, it was published in 1912, and as I handled the book my interest waned. Just as I was about to return both the copies to the bookseller I noticed the title of one of the chapters: 'In the Parish of Martaineszoy'. I sat down again and began to read. The bulk of the entry was about St Martin's Church and, to be fair to Black, he mostly kept his flowery language under control:

> *…An interesting structure and one of the most archi-tecturally important of the Level Churches, Norman in origin with later predominantly Fourteenth Century features. A three-stage tower with fine crenulations and a splendid spacious aisle with the stone screen a rare survival from circa 1360. There is even a small surviv-ing crypt with an intriguing 'underaisle' as the local people call it, whose destination is kept secret.*

If my appetite had been whetted by the photograph in the previous book, there was now a positive hunger to see the Church for myself. It gave an added incentive, if any were necessary, to my forthcoming meeting with the vicar of Martaineszoy, Patrick Monahan. But to my disappointment there was only a passing reference to the Hexagon as a 'Six-sided Folly, probably sixteenth century.' Despite this brevity I bought the book and said farewell to the jovial bookseller.

After I left England's smallest city the topography changed. Gone were the familiar undulating hills of the West Country and, as I descended, laid out before me was a plain. I stopped the car and got out to survey the scene. From my lofty perspective, the levels had the appearance of a vast green glacier making its way to the sea, sandwiched between the Mendips to the north and the Quantocks to the south. Only the low finger of the Polden Hills penetrated to its centre.

The flat landscape put me in mind of a mock-up such as one would find accompanying an elaborate planning proposal or a fancy model village. It was as if a draughtsman, presented with an horizontal plane, had divided the space into neat fields, their boundary hedges carefully demarked. Not content with that, our designer had inscribed the scene with dark drains or rhines, which flowed like veins through a body. I remembered from my research into Sedgemoor that these incursions are evidence of man's attempt, during the last two thousand years, to cheat the sea of its prize and produce rich farmland to cultivate. For most of the time this activity has been worthwhile, but every now and again, throughout history, natural forces have reminded its inhabitants that their tenure is conditional. Through the ages storms have inundated the land and returned this country-side to its primordial state.

From my vantage point I could see, too, that vestiges of the original marshes remained, exposed by stretches of water lined with billowing clumps of reed and bulrushes. Not all the landscape conformed to this uniform pattern; here and the plain was punctuated with mounds, better described as knolls. It was these remnants of another age, that were the original isles of this ancient floodplain. I delved into Black's book again and was intrigued and somewhat amused by his description of these 'isles'. The names of these were extravagant almost to the point of romance: Athleney – Island of the Princes, Greylake – Island of the Dead, Muchelney – The Great Island, Aller – Island of Mystery, Beckery – Holy Island, all of these I saw scattered across the expanse. I could now see how their elevation had been crucial to their survival. But, as you can imagine, my real interest was in locating the hill of Martaineszoy. For a moment I thought I could see something in the distance, but I could not be sure.

The road descended, and I found myself at last on the Levels themselves, in the midst of one of the most singular landscapes in England. I could now see close at hand the water meadows were enclosed by thick hedgerows which rose like bristles on a brush, giving the landscape its definition. I passed by the King's Sedgemoor drain and at once realised that I was near the site of the last pitched battle on English soil. I thought of the disastrous Monmouth rebellion and its aftermath, Jeffreys's Bloody Assize. By association, I journeyed even further back in time to the days when Alfred used this watery labyrinth as a refuge from the marauding Dane.

I parked the car and made my way along the path. Walking among these fields made me realise how the hedges, planted by man, have changed our perception of this landscape so that now these pastures unfold sequentially as you walk. Consequently, I found the experience became a series of revelations, each field its own world, emphasised by a devouring mist which hung low over the fields like a gigantic clammy hand. Where no hedges existed, however, the seemingly endless vistas to the sea deceived me into thinking that I was walking towards a cliff at the very edge of the world. In this misty setting distant figures assume the role of ghosts, discrete yet indistinct, as if they themselves had risen from this abyss.

As the path cut through a dense hedge, it was then that I saw it. Looming on a hilltop about a quarter of a mile in front of me was a dark shape, minatory, even at this distance. Emerging from its captive shroud of mist was the Martaineszoy Hexagon; a more surreal image would be hard to imagine. After a few paces I stopped again and, even as I stood spellbound before this strange sight, a malignant sun gave way to a grey and forbidding cloud. As the mist hugged the fields below, so the clouds glowered from above, as if elemental forces were combining to frame this lonely hill and its solitary feature for my benefit. The last of the sun's feeble rays were just enough to create a sinister silhouette of the building's elevation. In the past I have railed against those who have ascribed human attributes to inanimate objects … and yet … as I stood not fifty yards from the Hexagon, a disturbing presence seemed to be radiating from the very fabric of the building.

During my life and travels I had seen all manner and shape of buildings, but never had I encountered one in such an extraordinary position as that which lay ahead. The structure was perched in the centre of its elevated site, surrounded on all sides by a wide, flat plinth-like area of grass which led to a precipitous slope down to field level. Originally, as depicted in the drawing, a pitched roof of slate would have risen on each of its six sides to a point at its centre giving the building the appearance of a giant pencil which had been driven into the ground with just its tip remaining. This impression was not improved by the fact that the roof had long since disappeared, so that the jagged tops of the walls thrust skywards offering an open challenge to the heavens. In all, what remained of the structure was about thirty feet high and perhaps twenty-five feet or so across and, in its prime with a six-hipped roof, must have been an impressive sight. Facing me, built into one of the six elevations was a doorway, rather incongruously, given the lack of roof, filled by what appeared to be a stout oak door which was closed. Two windows were so placed either side and above the level of the door that they appeared as the eyes in a grotesque parody of the human face.

For an instant I thought I saw a shadow move by the door, a fleeting disturbance in the fading afternoon light. The moment passed but, as it did, a familiar sound rose up as if from the very fabric of the building itself. At first it was faint but then a relentless crescendo as the tolling filled the air. This time the resonance was clearer, it was like no bell I had ever heard before and, above all, I was certain that I was listening to a sound of great antiquity. As the ringing continued, an echo from down the centuries entered my head. It was merely a suggestion, nothing more, but something in the verses I found in the picture began to make sense. At first it seemed preposterous, but the more the idea took root the greater the possibility became. I struggled desperately to remember the narrative of an ancient legend, but I could only bring fragments of the story to mind. If I was right what lay at the heart of this affair belonged to the dawn of Christianity.

I started to shiver as the day grew cold and that ominous reverberation had started to echo around my head. I felt a sudden urge to return to the car but I was uneasy about turning my back on that grim edifice, especially as there was just the faint feeling that somehow I was being watched by whatever dwelt there.

By the time I reached the car, it was already past five o'clock and the autumn day was waning. I opened the door and with some relief settled into my seat. But something was wrong: a feeling, no more, which I tried to shrug off. I started the engine and instinctively checked the rear-view mirror. The instant I did so, I was paralysed. There, in the mirror was the figure from the picture. The satanic face, ice white, stared at me with lifeless eyes. Self-preservation gripped me, I fumbled at the door handle and fell out of the car. I ran up the track on which I had parked, letting out a declamatory yell, more in relief than fear. Anyone observing this extraordinary tableau would draw the conclusion that I was a madman. I stumbled to a halt about fifty yards from the car, and to my relief, I was not followed. I do not remember how long I stood there in the twilight, but it must have been a considerable time because I began to feel a distinct chill again. This discomfort, and the need for warmth, prompted me to reason that what I had experienced was merely a reaction to the sight of the Hexagon. So I made my way slowly back to the car with the aid of the torch, which I carried with me. As I approached my anxiety rose. I shone the torch but to my relief there was no sign of the figure. It was then I remembered that the picture was in the car with me and this, paradoxically, gave me some comfort. It seemed that its presence, in some way, provoked these apparitions. This is what I told myself, anyway.

Having recovered my composure, I consulted the map and after a couple of false starts I came in sight of Magnaveney House, just about visible in the murk. Its location was on rising ground at the edge of the Polden Hills and, as such, the position would have protected it from the worst of the flooding, hence why a house of this age had survived so well.

The building itself was substantial, two-storey, long and low with a pantile roof and whitewashed walls, looking westward to the sea. The curving, gravelled drive cut through extensive gardens and led to a superbly carved wooden porch. This elaborate structure was reminiscent of the kind of lych gate one might find at the entrance to church; fortunately, no coffin rested within it as I arrived. My host, looking more relaxed than he had done at his brother's funeral, opened the massive studded oak front door and came to greet me before I could get out of the car. He shook my hand vigorously, and picking up my case, said:

'So pleased you could come.'

I smiled and thanked him for inviting me. An unexpected pleasure awaited me when I went inside. Mrs Strickland turned out to be none other than Jessica Powell, the concert pianist. So much for her being 'some musician' as Baverstock had said. I remembered that she had not attended the funeral because of a bout of 'flu, which had left her still looking pale. Apart from that, in real life she was just as she appeared in her photographs: a tall, elegant woman with raven hair and a fine intelligent face, which bore an inquiring look as if she were in a constant state of comprehension. Her sensitive playing style had long been a favourite of mine and I had a number of her records in my collection. While she shook my hand I could feel her acute senses assessing my every expression and movement. An invisible bridge sprung up between us from the very beginning. There was mystery too, a part of her seemed unfathomable, unreachable as if she inhabited an entirely different plane of understanding from the rest of us.

The house had a simple layout, dictated by its elongated rectangular shape. An entrance hall with a staircase and straight passages on either side running the full length of the house with all the reception rooms, kitchen and cloakrooms leading off. The same pattern was repeated upstairs, with six bedrooms and two bathrooms accommodated. Despite its unsophisticated design there were bijou glories here and there. I counted three handsome inglenook fireplaces and some vestiges of the exquisite linenfold panelling which would originally have adorned many of the internal walls.

The couple seemed to live alone, apart from a housekeeper/cook, a widowed lady called Turley, who lived in a small cottage at the edge of the garden.

As I was unpacking and looking forward to a much needed bath, Strickland put his head round the door:

'Dinner at eight. I've invited Patrick Monahan, the vicar from Martaineszoy, he was a close friend of Harry's and we have both known him for a long time. You'll like him, he's quite the scholar, he … he knows much about Harry's research here.'

There was a gravity to his voice as he spoke these last words. The evening would be an interesting one, no doubt.

VII

During the meal I had the opportunity of getting to know Patrick Monahan and I found him instantly likeable. He was in his mid-forties, tall, with a rather grizzled appearance, untidy greying hair and a patient, considerate, rather studious, manner. He had the endearing habit of being a good listener and I imagined him to be a formidable man of letters. His voice, a soft Irish brogue, was one you would never tire of hearing.

The company was so receptive that I decided that this was the appropriate moment to tell them about my experiences both at Ashcombe and since encountering the drawing of the Martaineszoy Hexagon. When I told them about the fragment of Sir Simon's document which I had found in his namesake's desk, both Patrick and Jessica nodded thoughtfully as if this confirmed something they knew already. I was relieved to receive a sympathetic response to these revelations and, I have to admit, rather surprised. Instead of scepticism my extraordinary account of the last two years was greeted with the utmost understanding.

The normally inscrutable Christopher seemed to be wrestling with an inner conflict which caused him to lose concentration at times. It was clear to me that the trauma of HH's death had cast a great shadow over these people. This went beyond the expected grief of a family and close friends to what seemed to be a bewilderment about the mystery of his death. Or was it something more? Was their anxiety due to the fact that they knew the cause only too well and it scared them? In Patrick's case his anxiety was evident especially in unguarded moments when his otherwise impeccable concentration let him down. A frown would appear, as if some great struggle remained unresolved; at these moments he would withdraw from the conversation into a world far removed from the present. One thing was beyond doubt however, he would have much to contribute to the Martaineszoy affair when the time came.

After dinner we gathered in the sitting room. I was very pleased that Jessica joined us; she had shown throughout the evening to be someone of remarkable prescience and common sense. Christopher for his part was obviously keen to start. An expectant hush grew amongst us and I became aware too, of my own apprehension.

I had brought the drawing in with me and unwrapped it straight away. Both Christopher and Patrick leant forward to look, but Jessica refrained. I told them how I had deciphered the poem but decided not to make too much of my uncomfortable encounters so far. My only comment was to remark on its powerful presence; tellingly, Jessica looked straight at me and nodded perceptively. I wondered whether she'd had the same experience.

Christopher was the first to respond.

'What you've just demonstrated certainly makes sense of Harry's behaviour and his reaction. He showed us the writing before and after he had unravelled it. I have to confess that I thought it was an elaborate hoax by someone who had heard the history of the Hexagon and decided to exploit it for fun. But Harry was very excited about it and it now seems that he was right.'

At this point he shot a quick glance at Monahan, whose expression showed no sign of emotion.

'I always believed that Harry was right.' Jessica's voice was calm, but full of conviction. 'You see there is evil here, I have always sensed it. We should understand, before we go any further, that we are disturbing an age-old tension that runs deep through many of us. The Hexagon is what men have made it, a symbol of darkness which appeals to the basest instincts of the human race. Each of us has it within our nature to be enticed by such notoriety and poor Harry became increasingly obsessed with the place. Having known it all his life he was convinced there was some secret waiting to be unearthed. Then one day a few weeks ago he found the picture and, according to him, everything fell into place. It was strange really, he seemed both excited and … fearful. One thing I do know, the more one is exposed to that picture, the greater the effect of the real thing will be. I will not look at it, nor will I go near the place.'

Her voice was subdued; its tone was thoughtful and, I thought, full of nostalgic affection for her late brother-in-law.

'I don't suppose he revealed anything about just what had 'fallen into place.' I asked.

It was Christopher who replied.

'Alas no, Harry could be very secretive when he wanted to be, as I'm sure you know, Jack.'

'Or maybe he didn't want to expose any of you to any unnecessary risk,' said Monahan ominously. There was a strong conviction in his voice.

I could see Christopher wanted to deliver a serious rebuttal of Patrick's remark but instead made light of it.

'Well, Jack you'd better look out then as Harry clearly wanted to involve you,' he chuckled as he said it, but the laugh was hollow.

At this point I thought I detected a flicker of agreement from Monahan. Jessica's intervention had been extraordinary and utterly unexpected and Monahan's reaction was particularly interesting. It was as if he knew precisely what Jessica meant, and it troubled him.

There was an uncomfortable silence which was eventually broken by our host, who began:

'Between us, Jessica, Patrick and I hope to give you some of the background to the extraordinary story of the Martaineszoy Hexagon. Harry thought your family connections, the tragic events at Ashcombe and your sensitivity to, shall we say, uncanny matters, made your participation desirable.'

As he continued I was struck by Christopher's rather peremptory style which seemed out of step with the metaphysical subject matter, and to be honest it felt more like a general briefing his troops.

'As with many things the root of this lies deep in our history.'

'Actually Christopher, even further back than any of us may imagine', Patrick added.

'Let us come to that later, shall we?' Christopher said with just the hint of irritation in his voice, as if he had been interrupted unnecessarily. The world-weary diplomat made a fresh attempt to start his narrative.

'I should say at the outset that we have Harry to thank because his recent research has brought to light new insight into this tumultuous period in our history. In particular, he found two primary sources on the history of this part of Somerset and some hitherto unseen family papers. As a result, I can talk to you now with some confidence. Whether that has turned out to be good thing I will leave you to judge.'

'What I have to tell you is essentially a story of two men who lived two hundred years apart, and it saddens me to say that two blacker rogues never walked this earth. Jack, you are "acquainted", of course, with Sir Richard de Betancourt … rather too well I suspect!'

I nodded. He saw me wince as he said these words. Even after two years the very name sent shivers through my whole body.

'As you know only too well, Sir Richard died in 1457 in somewhat mysterious circumstances, a year after the murder of the hapless Sir Edward Cavendish. What you may not be aware of, however, is that it was he who built the Hexagon.'

This revelation took me completely by surprise. Old ghosts returned. Vivid images swirled in my head and once again I saw the faces of Abbot Roberte, of Edward Cavendish, of Brother Odo and most of all Sir Richard, himself.

'It seems I cannot escape him,' I said.

'Alas, Jack, in the affairs of the de Betancourts it is impossible to avoid him. Your account of the fragment of Sir Simon's mysterious puzzles confirms as much.'

I nodded in reluctant agreement.

'We are not certain of the exact date when the Hexagon was built, but piecing various sketchy documents together, the consensus is that it was completed by 1450. It seems to have been the personal whim of Sir Richard and an idea born of sheer evil.'

There was an acidic edge to his voice.

'But I am getting ahead of myself. I mentioned that there were two protagonists in our story and I should now introduce the second. You see, as well as the ubiquitous de Betancourt family, the Stricklands have also owned land here on the Levels for as long as any of us are able to establish, and certainly since the beginning of the fifteenth century. Their heyday came in the aftermath of the Civil War and the Commonwealth. Through careful alliances and marriages the estate was increased to many thousands of acres, here and in the Mendips. The Strickland name was one to be both feared and respected throughout the land, from the humblest circles to the highest ranks of the royal court. Nothing, it seems, could stop the inexorable rise of our family, but out of an apparently endless clear blue sky a dark shadow appeared. That shadow took the form of Sir Thomas Strickland, who inherited the land and titles in 1674. It saddens me to say that I am a descendant of his; he possessed many of the vices that come with money and power – gambling, drinking, and womanising – which he practised to an excessive degree.

Ever since you discovered that we Stricklands are related to the de Betancourts you must have been wondering how that came about. Well, I can tell you that Sir Thomas lies at the heart of it all. You see he was a direct descendant of Sir Richard de Betancourt, through his mother. I'll return to this villain shortly, but first I should tell you what we know about the Hexagon and its origins.

'Not that there was a Hexagon, of course, when Sir Richard inherited the title and lands of the de Betancourts in the middle of the fifteenth century, but merely a bare mound, similar to many such geological features on the Levels. I say "bare", although there were thought to be the remnants of a much older stone structure on the site. We do not know this for sure because there has, to my knowledge, never been an archaeological excavation. In those days, the site was just known as Martaineszoy or Martin's Island. We need to remember that the Levels appear as they do today because of the continuing efforts to drain the marshes for over a thousand years. Even now this can be a precarious place and without proper maintenance flooding is a constant threat. You might have expected that a bare hillock like Martaineszoy, to be an unexceptional example of what was a common feature of the landscape, but the various histories will tell you that it has always had a sinister reputation. All sorts of nefarious activities are supposed to have taken place there and, although much of this was just the superstitious gossip of country folk, the stories persisted. For instance, one such legend is that no trees will grow there.'

I thought of the ominous line in the verse, '… *Atop a hille without a tree …*'

'As we already know, Richard was a man drawn to the darker side of existence. Doubtless he absorbed the legends surrounding Martin's Island and became fascinated by them. He certainly seems to have spent an inordinate amount of time there, disproportionally so considering the size of his vast estate. Admittedly, the de Betancourt lands here on the levels possessed a comfortable manor house in those days but, even so, this was something of an outpost of his domain. So, for a restless soul like Richard, there had to be a compelling reason for him to occupy his time there. One of the intriguing things to emerge from Harry's research was that Richard was said to have spoken about 'a discovery of import' there. Until recently, we have had no idea what this was but now …'

At this point he glanced again at Patrick who this time gave him a knowing look in return.

'Richard decided, for whatever reason, to erect a building on Martaineszoy. Perhaps his discovery was something so important that it confirmed the sinister reputation of the place and merited a memorial of some kind, something he could exploit. From what I have learnt about the man, he does not strike me as someone who was particularly motivated by religion or heresy; he was too busy indulging in other vices to be distracted by affairs of the church or other, how shall I say, beliefs. It is quite possible, of course, that Richard used his possession of this mysterious object to strike fear into the local population and reinforce his authority. Whatever his private reasons, the public justification for this indulgence was that the estate needed a folly, a landmark, to give aesthetic pleasure to the eye. Given the dark history of Martin's Hill and Richard's own character you can imagine that his idea gave rise to renewed speculation, so what rose from this barren site outraged some and delighted others. One thing everyone could agree on: the Martaineszoy folly was a striking addition to the landscape.

'But it did not take long for certain conclusions to be drawn about its design, conclusions which made local people cross themselves in fear. The building, as we know, was a hexagon built in the darkest stone that Richard could lay his hands on, with a roof of six hips to match the construction of the walls. But that was not all. Inside, around the central axis, another, much narrower, six-sided structure was created, reflecting the shape of the outer walls, to act as a pier holding up the roof. Six narrow windows, one for each face, were included in the outside walls as well as a gothic style doorway. The whole was not large, but its design and position gave it an air of imposition rarely achieved by structures of this modest size. Ostensibly, it was a building to look at rather than inhabit, not that many were to be tempted inside. It did not take long for lurid tales to take hold. The most powerful of these came from those who saw an underlying diabolical design to all this. One contemporary historian expressed it in colourful language: six external walls, six windows and six internal walls – 666, the mark of the Beast.

'We should not forget that the Hexagon is to some extent a palimpsest; built supposedly over the vestiges of a much earlier building. As I said earlier we have no knowledge of what came before, only hearsay. But in some way we might imagine Richard's construction as both a continuation and a catalyst for whatever practices took place on Martin's Hill. The only other fragment which comes down to us seems to imply that, whatever it was that he discovered there, he did not remove it, which implies that its intrinsic value may be low, instead as the document which Harry found says "*He toucheth ne that whiche layeth therein.*"'

Christopher sighed before continuing.

'It seems that Sir Thomas Strickland did not suffer from the same reticence, as we shall see. Which brings us to our egregious forbear. Thomas was the eldest son of Sir William Strickland and Matilda de Betancourt, so inheriting the baronetcy. As I said before, the Strickland estate in those days was large but not so extensive as to include the land on which the Hexagon stood, which came as part of Matilda's dowry. If ever one needed an explanation for the concentration of wealth and power in aristocratic families, one need look no further than the institution of marriage. Occasionally, no doubt, such matches were underpinned by the pretence of love, but most of the time, it seemed, the principal purpose was to increase the capital and land of the respective parties. I may be cynical, but I believe this was the prime consideration in the case of Sir William Strickland and Matilda de Betancourt. Just how much land came from the latter source is unknown, but the critical point, as far as we are concerned, this is how the Hexagon came to be a part of the Strickland estate.'

'Yes, I see,' I said, 'it certainly helps to explain HH's bequest to Em. Who would have thought that a marriage over three hundred years ago would have such consequences for the present.'

But it was Jessica again who made the telling intervention.

'Have you considered that Harry's motives might have been more complex than you think?

At this point she glanced at Christopher as if to seek approval for what she was about to say.

'How so?' I was intrigued.

'You need to understand Harry's frame of mind in those last days. He was a changed man, as I have said. He was fearful, fearful, that is, for his life. He said to me that he was so glad that he had already made arrangements to leave his picture collection to you *especially* in the light of events. Remember too, that he knew of your success in solving the puzzle at Ashcombe, it was this that made him suspect that you were the innocent spoken of in Sir Simon's document.'

'But how could he know of Sir Simon's prophecy? It was hidden away in Simon's desk at Ashcombe when I found it.'

Jessica took a deep breath.

'Now is the time to tell you the secrets that Harry shared with us about the de Betancourt legend. I can tell you now that it was Harry who uncovered Sir Simon's document in the Bodleian. Harry knew Simon's father, they were almost contemporaries after all, so when he found the papers he knew that he should send copies to Ashcombe. I'm sure Harry's connection with the family was known to Simon's father but, just as he had done with you, he did not want this revealed, especially as Simon was up at College. He just felt that their association would be compromised. Harry was like that; he hated his fellow academics knowing his business and he guarded his privacy jealously. At the time Harry thought little more about the discovery, true he found it intriguing but suspected too, like Christopher, that it might be an elaborate hoax. It wasn't until after Simon had inherited Ashcombe, and the unearthing of Brother Odo's book together with your solution of the puzzle it contained, that he began to believe that the document might be authentic. The discovery of the Hexagon drawing with the likelihood that this was the second of Sir Simon's 'tests' confirmed Harry's suspicion. In particular he was sure by then of your importance in the de Betancourt story and that the time had come to involve you, warn you even. It was the potential risk involved that finally persuaded him. Even then he was worried that to make you aware of the curse might compromise your "state of innocence" as he called it. He had no idea, of course, that you had already seen Sir Simon's document.'

'Why on earth didn't Harry set about solving the conundrum himself after its discovery?' I asked.

'Don't you see? Harry believed in the legend; he realised that he was not the person spoken of by Sir Simon. After all he had found the original document and knew all about the so-called curse, hardly the status of an innocent. To interfere might jeopardise the whole thing. As it happened he was vindicated considering the course of events at Ashcombe. I have no idea whether Simon had spoken to Harry or even knew of his connection with the family after he had discovered the first puzzle. Though it is interesting to hear you say though that Em was unaware of the ties with Harry. Whatever the truth, I suspect Simon already had plans. Ask yourself this: is it too fanciful to suggest that he had some awareness of your importance from the very first moment he met you, something innate, passed down to him through the centuries? I believe in such things.'

I was stunned by these new revelations. The irony of my friendship with Harry, when all the time we unconsciously shared parts of the same secret, was one thing, but to have Simon's duplicity exposed was almost too much for me to take in. There could be little doubt that his behaviour was testament to Sir Simon's warning of a recurrent sickness in the de Betancourt line. My betrayal at the hands of Simon at Ashcombe was something I had brushed off as an aberration on his part, but hearing what Jessica had to say, it looked as though I had been used as a pawn from the word go. Now that I look back, there was something strange about the curious way that Simon would look at me from time to time at Oxford, his keenness to cultivate my friendship and the way in which I was taken into his circle of friends. The moment that Brother Odo's book was discovered became the trigger for the invitation for me to visit Ashcombe for the first time, on the pretext of cataloguing the library. A sense of bleakness enveloped me and yet not for a moment did I consider abandoning the bizarre quest which had so preoccupied me.

Both Jessica and Christopher realised the effect of her words were having on me and as I struggled to respond, Jessica put her hand on my arm. But it was Christopher who spoke:

'This must be difficult for you Jack, but I hope you see why it was imperative that we invite you here. Whether or not you give any credence to these matters is, of course, up to you, but we felt you had to know. Especially considering your closeness to Harry.'

'Yes, I do understand entirely and thank you for being so frank. I freely admit this comes as something of a shock, but not entirely. When I discovered Sir Simon's document I must admit the thought that I might be the innocent spoken of in the premonition briefly flashed across my mind. I soon dismissed the whole idea as fantasy, but like everything else in this affair I never cease to be amazed by the turn of events. I suppose the fact that someone as rational as Harry took this seriously rather brings it home to me.'

Outside the wind rattled the window ominously.

Christopher ignored the interruption.

'Would it be appropriate for me to continue? What comes next may help to put matters in perspective ...'

'Please do', I said, relieved at the prospect of moving on.

'If you remember, I was talking about the marriage of Matilda de Betancourt and now might be the moment to consider the nature of this matriarchal figure. Matilda was a direct descendant of Richard and there seems to be little doubt that Thomas's aberrations, and there were many, have their origin in this bloodline. The spirit of Richard, if you can call it that, had found its way into the Strickland dynasty, much as Sir Simon feared it would in that document you found, Jack. By all accounts she was vindictive, cruel and utterly ruthless; by contrast, her husband was passive and retiring. One particular episode speaks of a servant accused of stealing and other crimes; Matilda not only insisted that he hang but she demanded the Tyburn Tree method, whereby the unfortunate victim does not have his neck broken instantly by a drop but is hauled into the air and left to dance, prolonging the agony. She was not a woman to cross, that's certain. All these attributes, and more, Thomas inherited from his mother, but he had one evil obsession, far worse even than any of these, one which affected his very soul.'

At this point he paused. It was an electric moment. From down the centuries I sensed a darkness, an invisible pall descended on us all. Nobody spoke. An instinctive reaction caused me to re-cover the picture which lay in front of us still. They all knew why.

'Now Jack, have you ever studied paganism or the dark arts in the course of your research?'

The question came as quite a surprise.

'No, not directly, although during this free term I had planned to delve into arcane writing and its application. In particular I'm interested in how spies and heretics used codes and ciphers in the medieval and renaissance periods to communicate with each other. I think it is bound to touch on, shall we say, certain esoteric practices.' I replied.

'No wonder you were able to decipher the verses then. Let's say I'm now going to "touch on" some "esoteric practices" that will surprise you. Heaven forbid that the blood of the main protagonist flows in my veins too, but that is the curse we Stricklands have to live with. You will know, of course, that in the medieval world the idea of a Nature deity and Christianity sat rather uneasily together; remember that the latter supplanted the former as the dominant system of belief, and old habits die hard and long. The change took place over many centuries as both creeds frequently co-existed, sometimes even using the same symbols and myths. This was especially so in rural communities like ours, where the presence of Nature and its power over people is at its most prevalent. These people lived with the wonders of creation every day and were entirely comfortable with a life led in tune with the seasons, the eternal cycle of death and renewal. Well, it seems this area has a particularly rich history of such belief.'

During this peroration, Monahan seemed to accept the ecclesiastical implications of what was being said. I watched him carefully. There was a keen intelligence about his face and a barely suppressed sense of urgency. But, as at dinner, there was, I thought, a great weight on him.

Christopher continued.

'You might expect that by the end of the seventeenth century the influence of the Orthodox Church would have extinguished much of this heterogeneity. But you'd be wrong. There is an old saying in these parts: "Christianity in public and heresy in private."'

Monahan smiled ruefully at this remark.

'It was quite feasible for someone to espouse both beliefs without demur. Pockets of devil worship, covens of witches and paganism were all celebrated as guilty pleasures.

'It seems that Thomas wasted little time in putting the tower to use. If the stories about Martaineszoy which had come down to us from history before the Hexagon was built were bad enough, the tales of what went on there during his time reached fever pitch.

Just like his egregious forbear, from an early age he became utterly consumed by the place and no one could understand why. Some thought he had a special, even spiritual affinity with the Hexagon, others that he just had a fascination with evil. Whatever the truth, Thomas recognised that this was a site of enormous importance to the followers of the old religion. When he wasn't drinking or whoring, he would spend hours there in a trance-like state as if in rapture of some kind. Rumours about his activities began to reach fanciful levels; so much so that there were fears that the Black Sabbath was celebrated regularly at the dead of night, and it was widely believed Thomas was in daily communion with the Devil. Not that he was alone. He had surrounded himself with a coterie of followers of the most venal kind. These men were the very worst of humanity: dissolute and utterly amoral; no depravity was beyond them. One of the more oblique mysteries surrounded the evidence that someone, the implication being Thomas himself, had been excavating inside the Hexagon itself. What the purpose of this might have been no one knew, but that did not stop people from gossiping. He was by now claiming that he had discovered its 'spiritual' significance. He announced that he was in possession of evidence to this effect, in the shape of an artefact of unimaginable power which he had unearthed at the site. Whether this was merely an apocryphal smokescreen, or a secret shared with his most trusted friends we shall never know; but one thing is certain, he never revealed its secret publicly.

Parallels were drawn with the discovery in Richard's time and soon these rumours were embellished with the idea that buried treasure had been found. Suffice to say that it was around this time that Thomas's interest in the Hexagon became evermore intense. It was almost that he had been vindicated in some way and that now the place had assumed a 'religious' significance in his eyes.

Monahan shot me a glance; words were unnecessary. It seemed that Christopher was now reaching the climax of his story.

'It is highly possible,' he added, 'that disaster at the hands of the Church Authorities and, who knows, the civil law too, would have overtaken Thomas if it hadn't been for a chance encounter with his distant cousin, Charlotte de Betancourt, who came from a very different branch of the family from his mother.'

He paused and looked at me.

'You see, Jack, from a tangle of relationships our paths have already crossed irrevocably. The bond that Cartwright spoke of between the de Betancourts and the Stricklands has, as you will see, a double connection. I could never understand why Harry was so coy about it with you, much better to have said something. It would have been a new focus for your relationship, given that he was already fond of you. Anyway, that is by the by.'

I was somewhat embarrassed by what he said and relieved when he ploughed on with his narrative.

'In many ways Charlotte seems to be just about the best thing that happened in Thomas's blighted existence. It is a miracle that the two ever got together. History does not record what brought this about, but perhaps this was yet another marriage based on purely mercenary considerations. It is easy to see why Charlotte would be an attractive partner for our errant forbear; she was an heiress in her own right to a considerable part of the de Betancourt fortune, with the bonus that she seemed to be endowed with all the good sense so lacking in her prospective husband. At the time of their betrothal Thomas had continued his heretical ways serving two faiths, until Charlotte, who was a devout Christian, got wind of his 'complicated' devotional arrangements. She soon issued her husband-to-be with an ultimatum: "sever your links with these heathens or forget any thoughts of marriage." Well, our Charlotte must have been some lady, because Thomas did not hesitate to fall in with her demands. Being a cynic at heart I guess that, however exquisite her charms may have been, the fact that she brought a large dowry to the marriage, just as his mother had done, meant that Thomas, whose moral compass was, shall we say, somewhat erratic, had a powerful practical reason to agree. Within a short space of time Thomas appeared to be a reformed character; something which I suspect came as a shock to both his committed followers and sharpest critics alike.

'After their marriage in 1681, there began a period of consolidation of the Strickland estates, no doubt encouraged by his new bride, in which all manner of improvements were made. One symbol of Thomas's past remained however: the Martaineszoy Hexagon. It's hard to know now what Charlotte felt about this notorious landmark which she would have seen every day from the old medieval house, now long gone, destroyed by fire in the eighteenth century. Yet the Hexagon survives, albeit without its roof. Rather fancifully, I like to think Charlotte saw the apparently redundant Hexagon as proof that the new Christian regime, which she had been so instrumental in bringing about, had triumphed over Paganism.

'But three years into their marriage, during which Charlotte bore him two sons, there came a sudden *volte face.* There is, I think, something deep in the psyche of a man like Thomas Strickland which cannot resist the lure of the exotic and the amoral. It seems he had tired of his wife's constricting piety and once again sought the company of his old cronies, who relished the opportunity to resume their former ways. The Hexagon again became the focus for evil. But this time it was different: Thomas had a wife whose power and influence were every bit his equal. With the backing of her family, she took the extraordinary step of publicly denouncing him in church as, not merely an unbeliever, but a disciple of Satan. Such was the weight attached to the de Betancourt family's word, corroborated by many local people who had tired of his ways, that Thomas would surely have been tried for heresy and burnt at the stake had not fate taken a different course.

'If I tell you that the year was 1685, you will know instantly what I'm talking about. It is a date etched into the hearts of many families hereabouts, even today. Prince James, Duke of York, had become King of England on the death of his elder brother, Charles II, on 6th February, 1685. As you undoubtedly know, James II was a Catholic and resented by powerful Protestants under his rule. Well, the focus for much of this dissent was James Scott, Duke of Monmouth, the eldest illegitimate son of Charles II, who was persuaded to claim the throne. I'm sorry, talk about telling your grandmother to suck eggs! You know all this don't you!'

'No please carry on; I'm very interested in the local context of your narrative in the wider history', I said.

'Well, if you're sure. So Monmouth landed at Lyme Regis

in June 1685 and in the following few weeks he rallied a growing army of nonconformists, artisans and farm workers to his cause. Not many were professional soldiers, and that was to be his undoing. For Thomas, the rebellion came as a godsend, the distraction he needed with the authorities breathing down his neck. Monmouth was just kind of figure to attract our reprobate: daring, passionate and reckless, to boot. I think we can safely discount the cause of Protestantism as a reason, given his predilections! So he threw in his lot with the handsome adventurer, which action brought him much praise locally and temporary relief from his accusers. The fate of the rebellion you will know. Having fought a number of skirmishes with local militias and regular soldiers and failing to capture the city of Bristol, it ended with the defeat of Monmouth's army at the Battle of Sedgemoor on 6th July 1685, very close to where we are sitting now. By this time, as you can imagine, Charlotte had long since removed Thomas's two sons to a place of safety. We do not know where, but my guess is a de Betancourt house somewhere not too far away. Perhaps even Ashcombe.'

He paused. Clearly what he was about to say next meant something to him, his eyes were cast down. Curious. After a minute's silence, he resumed.

'You can imagine the chaos in the hours after the battle. Men, good men, were hunted down. Soon trees here were adorned with hanging corpses; some say that these summary executions resulted in as many as half a dozen rebels swinging from the same bough. It was carnage, justice meted out on the hoof. Thomas, having been one of the cheerleaders for Monmouth and therefore a special prize, was sought everywhere. As the days passed it seemed that our mercurial ancestor had eluded his captors. In truth, he had hidden as Alfred had done centuries earlier, in the marshes. He had the advantage of knowing the area well and there were few places that had escaped his attention. One by one his followers were captured and put to death, until only Thomas remained, but eventually his luck ran out. The King's men caught up with him at … the Hexagon.'

All paths seemed to lead back to this strange building.

'Some say that he was betrayed by the vicar of Martaineszoy, but nothing was ever proven …

Monahan looked a little discomforted by this but nonetheless continued to pay close attention to our host.

'…Anyway he was brought for trial before the Bloody Assize, but ominously for Thomas, the Church intervened at his trial. This was the moment when his past overtook him. So appalled was the court by the allegations that they turned him over to his accusers, for them to prescribe such punishment as the Ecclesiastical Authorities saw fit. The Church certainly extracted a terrible revenge; Thomas was condemned to be buried alive. A death too awful to contemplate, even for a reprobate. The most curious thing was, according to those who were present, he showed not one iota of distress. His last words before he lapsed into a rapturous state were "You will never destroy me for I shall be part of you, that which you would rather forget." But his executioners just laughed and, as a last gesture of ridicule, hung about his neck the precious object he had discovered. But even as they scoffed, some said they never forgot the look he gave them: it was almost as if they were gazing into the eyes of Satan himself. One of the great ironies of this story is that the Church authorities clearly had no idea of the significance of Thomas's discovery.

'Ever since, a great mystery has surrounded the whereabouts of his body. In one sense you can understand why his accusers would want to keep the location to themselves, to prevent it becoming a shrine for the ungodly. The obvious place, which at least had the authentic ring of poetic justice about it, was the Hexagon, of course. Down the centuries people have dug up parts of the floor but to no avail and so the secret has remained hidden. That is until now … and that's where the drawing comes in.'

At this point, he paused and looking straight at Monahan, he said:

'That's enough of me droning on, I think it best if you take up the story from here, Patrick.'

I had been so mesmerised by Christopher's revelations that the abrupt ending took me by surprise. The cleric who, like me, had been the model of concentration, stiffened, looking slightly lost for a second and then eventually picked up the threads. All the while Jessica seemed in something of a trance, passive and yet in her eyes there was unease.

Monahan began.

'Harry and I shared a deep interest in the local history here. What I have to tell really begins with Harry's discovery of the picture in the Oxford gallery. In all the years I've known him I've never seen him so excited. It was only a few days after buying it that he came down to Somerset and already he'd revealed its mysteries. When he showed it to me, he said:

"Don't you see; this confirms what we both thought about the secret of the Hexagon?"

'I asked him, "how do we know?" This made him really impatient with me:

"Read the bloody verses man, it's obvious. This drawing and the verses are of sixteenth century origin and were clearly produced by someone who had discovered the secret and left it for future generations to discover."

He went on to tell me about his discovery of the Sir Simon fragment and how he now linked it with your experience in the library at Ashcombe.

'It now seems likely that Harry was not only right, but that the riddle in the picture is the work of the great Sir Simon. It is in all likelihood, as he said, the second of his three conundrums. Anyway, whatever the truth of it, Harry believed the object in question to be something of incredible importance and said that he was going to see for himself.

'I tried to point out to him that although the family still own the building it was now a scheduled ancient monument and shouldn't be defaced, but he wasn't listening. Anyway, I didn't hear from him until two days later when he came to the vicarage looking haggard and careworn. He seemed to have aged many years in that time. There was desperation in his voice when he said:

"I was right, but I sensed a powerful malediction. On reflection, I think it is best left alone."'

I intervened, 'He said something similar to his scout at College.'

'Yes, I'm sure it worried him. I was going to suggest …' His voice tailed away as if he was unsure of himself.

'Yes?' I said trying to prompt him.

'I should explain that since my student years, first at Trinity [Dublin, that is] and then Oxford where I met Harry, I have researched Irish history and I think I was some help to Harry in unravelling this mystery. I now have an idea what might lie at the bottom of all this, but it is so incredible that I need to make sure before I say anything.'

'Ah, Irish history, I have some ideas about that, but I suspect there is more,' I said.

'Oh, you'd be surprised. When I suggested that Harry and I return to Martaineszoy, his reply was unexpected and puzzling:

"No, we must involve a young colleague of mine, Jack Tregarden. In a way this is his story and, although he doesn't know it yet, what happened to him two years ago is far from over yet."

'I had no idea who or what he was talking about then, but as he seemed so insistent, I went along with what he said. Hence you're here now.'

Monahan couldn't have known the full impact of HH's

words, but at that moment it was clear to me that I must pursue the truth wherever it led me. Then he went on:

'Anyway, I was going to suggest that you and I meet at the Hexagon tomorrow afternoon and try out my theory. I'm sorry I can't make it before about five as I have a funeral to conduct, but I can come soon afterwards. It's an easy short cut across the meadows from the church.'

It was on this disquieting note that the evening ended.

VIII

The next day dawned without sun; instead, vast grey armies made their way in haste across the sky. The trees were unable to resist the wind from the east and they swayed and groaned reluctantly. The stillness of the last few days had gone, the wind had begun to stir on the previous evening and now it felt that the weather itself was a harbinger of change. This was an ominous wind, it insinuated itself into every nook and cranny. It brought colder air that discomforted, a gloomier light that disheartened, and a howl that cautioned; something troubling rode this relentless interloper.

I got up slowly and spent the day reading about the local history, browsing some of the books that Christopher had undoubtedly used as the basis for last night's narration. Christopher himself had gone into Taunton for the morning but would return for lunch, which meant that I had the pleasure of listening to Jessica practise. The music drifted to the room where I sat and at times all I could do was to stop reading and let the sound engulf me. She was playing that *tour de force* for the piano, 'Pictures at an Exhibition' by Mussorgsky, which was composed as a 'A Remembrance of Viktor Hartmann', the painter. When she reached 'The Old Castle', the haunting chords transported me to the ruin of the Martaineszoy Hexagon. In my mind's eye I could see the curious jagged outline and the strange hill on which it was built. It seemed to me that its secret was as mysterious as the music I was listening to. The thought occurred that her choice of this piece might not have been entirely accidental. Perhaps Jessica too was reliving the resurrection of the Hexagon's story and the distress it clearly caused.

Despite the unwelcome associations the music invoked, the playing was wonderful. There is something uniquely thrilling about being in the company of such a gifted human being. So the morning passed in intermittent reverie punctuated by the events of Sedgemoor and the infamous Thomas Strickland. I pondered the latter's life and his appalling death – just what was it that he had discovered that made him 'sanctify' such a bleak feature as Martaineszoy? Whether it was the spell of the music or my overactive imagination, but as the morning progressed, a conviction took hold of me so strongly as to be overpowering, that today I would find out the answer to that question. Far from satisfying my curiosity I found the prospect chilling.

Over lunch Jessica seemed particularly anxious and distracted. When we had finished she gripped my arm saying:

'For God's sake be careful this afternoon. No amount of learning can protect you from this.'

Without waiting for a reply she turned away to resume her practice. I can see the fear in her face even now.

Christopher handed me the key to the Hexagon with a knowing look and I left Magnaveney just after half past three to walk the two miles to Martaineszoy. It was relatively easy going across the levels and it meant that I had the opportunity to see more of this strange country. Monahan had invited me to supper after our excursion and a bed for the night at the vicarage which lay in the hamlet of Martaineszoy, no more than half a mile from the Hexagon. As I walked I was aware of the nagging east wind once more and thought of the old country rhyme 'When the wind is in the east, 'tis no good for man or beast'. As the path led me beside a wide rhine the wind first teased, then ruffled the surface, so that the waves darted in irregular patterns: the unfathomable chaos of the east wind. I remembered that Jarndyce uses it several times in 'Bleak House' as a harbinger of unfavourable events; 'I'll take an oath it's either in the east or going to be. I am always conscious of an uncomfortable sensation now and then when the wind is blowing in the east.' This thought gave me little comfort.

This was not a day for birds who inhabit the water. The ducks, coots and geese had all retreated to the shelter of the margins where tall reeds offered sanctuary. Not a swan could be seen anywhere. Such cattle as were still grazing these erstwhile summer pastures had huddled together in forlorn groups under low lying branches. It seemed that the whole world was in hiding from this disquieting day; I did not see another soul as I made my way. But something was coming.

As I emerged from a stile in a thick, high hedge, there was Martaineszoy, glowering at me in the increasing haze. No sooner had I been confronted by it than the rain started. At first, the random drops were apologetic, but within minutes they were reinforced and whipped against my face in a stinging rebuke. The torrent fell from a sky now livid, its indiscriminate volleys flattening grass, flooding paths and threatening chaos. Such weather conjures visions of the apocalypse, the end of days, bringing fear as its willing accomplice. Suddenly the haven of shelter beckoned, even if it meant entering the Hexagon alone. For once, the ringing in my ears that had blighted my existence in recent days was the least of my concerns. I started to run towards the building while fumbling for the key to the door. Even though it was roofless, I could at least get inside away from the harassment of the wind. I scrambled up the now slippery hillside ignoring as best I could the oppressive facade. Close up, the door was an impressive piece of work, solid black oak and, although weathered, would have easily withstood the most determined intruder. As I struggled to put the key in the lock I hesitated; the wind, now at gale force, launched a concerted attack, whistling through the slit windows and firing arrows of rain against the stonework. Although my desire to see what lay inside the walls overcame my reluctance, deep down I had no doubt that there was evil here. To make matters worse there was still no sign of Monahan, and the light was fading.

The door groaned in sympathy with the elements as I pushed it open. I looked inside without entering. If the light outside was dying, inside it was already moribund. I peered earnestly round the doorway in the gloom, towards Martaineszoy Church hoping to see Monahan, but to no avail. At least the rain had eased, but the wind if anything, had increased. With anxiety levels rising, I decided to immerse myself in the mysteries of the Hexagon. By now it was pretty well dark and although I had brought a powerful torch with me it somehow failed to illuminate the interior as much as I had hoped. Nonetheless I could see that the open space before me surrounded a remarkable central feature. This latter construction, as Christopher had explained the previous evening, was a hexagonal pillar, although it was considerably larger than that term would imply. It mirrored the outer walls and ran all the way up to the point of the roof apex. Like the external facade the stone had been carefully ashlared and it was obvious that a lot of care had gone into the initial building work. I walked around the central column and, considering the fact that it had been open to the elements for over a hundred years, it was in good condition. Some consolidation work had been carried out to the top, so that water could not penetrate the core, but even with this the preservation was remarkable.

As I moved I shone the torch on the stonework asking myself just what was it that HH had discovered here? I could see nothing suggestive at all – the floor had certainly not been disturbed and nothing else seemed awry. My mind raced, searching for a clue, but the only tangible evidence I had was the enigmatic verse. It must have led HH to the truth somehow. I recited it again and again to myself dissecting every line, analysing every word. Just as I was about to give up, an extraordinary idea entered my head, that I immediately tried to dismiss. But it wouldn't disappear:

Then here forever will I stay

Outside the wind shrieked as if in disbelief at my idea. Once again I examined the stonework, only this time it was with more care. Several minutes passed before I found what I was looking for and, with it, the cause of HH's fear. Opposite the door, in the middle of one of the six sides at head height, the stonework showed signs of recent disturbance. It was only slight and had been replaced with great care, but it was there, nonetheless. The prospect made my blood run cold, but my curiosity got the better of me. One large stone was still just proud of the others and with a little persuasion I managed to pull it towards me. Slowly it grated with its neighbours and, after what seemed an interminable amount of time, came free. But as it did the stone above fell out too, narrowly missing my foot and hitting the floor with a sickening thud. I realised that HH must have removed that one as well. The dust swirled round the opening and I shone the torch into the darkness. Never shall I forget the sight that greeted me, despite having anticipated it. There, right in front of my face was the eyeless stare of a skull.

As I recoiled from the shock my torch shone into the void and revealed the unnatural position of the arms which were stretched out either side of the hapless skeleton. It seems they were secured in some way to a large standing stone around which the building had been erected. Were these the mortal remains of the infamous Thomas Strickland? He hadn't been *buried* alive as such, but rather in the manner of the luckless Fortunato in 'The Cask of Amontillado'. In an horrific twist of irony the Hexagon had become his tomb. The very thought of such a death filled me with such revulsion that for a moment I could not catch my breath. But there was something else. Slung around his neck was another chain, badly decomposed, which clearly held an object hanging below the margins of the opening in the stonework. Having partially recovered my equilibrium I reached over tentatively to see if I could grasp whatever it was. The wording of the verses was ringing in my ears:

'... *I now holde what they all seeke*
Never touch it come what may
Else dearely learne to rew the day'

Suddenly a light flashed in my face and a voice roared: 'For God's sake don't touch it!

I swivelled round and there in the doorway stood Patrick Monahan. My relief was palpable.

'Thank God you're here!'

'I see you have confirmed my theory for me. I presume you'd figured it out too.'

'Well, yes I just recalled the verses, but if this is Thomas Strickland, how come Sir Simon was able to write about this a hundred and fifty years before it happened?'

He shone his torch into the void. The sight made him quail visibly.

'Because it's more complicated than that. The object which adorns Thomas ... like you I'm pretty sure that this is him ... wasn't always round his neck; before that it was in the possession of another. It is this individual whose story we are now part of, just as Sir Richard de Betancourt and then Sir Thomas Strickland once were, although I hasten to add our motivation is very different! Don't worry about this now, I'll explain as much as I know when we get back to the vicarage. I dare say you have some ideas yourself.'

'A few,' I replied.

Monahan looked again at the menacing grin on the head of the skull.

'Poor devil. No matter what his heresies were, he did not deserve to die like this. Sometimes, I despair at the cruelties this church of mine has been responsible for down the ages.'

His face was racked with the tension that lay between sorrow and anger.

'We have moved on', I said in consolation.

'Have we?'

Before I could answer him, he said:

'The time has come to set matters straight; heaven knows it's been long enough. What you see here is just a small part of an epic story.'

With that and without warning he plunged his arm into the opening and pulled up the chain that hung so precariously about Thomas Strickland. I moved to stop him, but he motioned me away:

'Don't worry Jack, I'm wearing the cross: I'll come to no harm.'

As Monahan removed the chain an object slowly emerged from the darkness, bulkier than I had expected. I heard him mutter a word of satisfaction as if his expectations had been met, at the same time gone was the boisterous wind to be replaced by an eerie stillness. Whatever was coming had arrived.

The first hint that something was wrong came from a shuffling sound from somewhere inside the building. Because of the unaccustomed silence I could hear it very distinctly and my initial thought was that a rat had emerged from its nest. But it wasn't a rat. Instead the noise modulated into an irregular breathing as of someone struggling to break free from a deep slumber. A very deep slumber. Enhanced by the light of our torches a monstrous shadow rose from the earth and towered over us covering the walls like some foul distemper. It was impossible to make out a distinct shape, but the menace was visceral. All the while the skull grinned at us in the ghastly, pale light, as if satisfied that some ancient rite was now to be fulfilled.

Monahan acted quickly. He now had in his hand the object which for three centuries had adorned the festering corpse of Thomas Strickland.

'Quick Jack, we must run for the Church,' his voice cracking with fear.

Without further thought we both made for the doorway, slithered down the hillside and with the aid of torchlight sought the sanctuary of St. Martin's Church. As soon as we had made level ground I could not resist looking back at the Hexagon. I soon regretted that. Something, I know not what, emerged from the open doorway. Already it was making its way down the slope towards us. As we fled for our lives across the fields, I could sense its overwhelming presence behind us, the sickening stench of death becoming stronger with every stride. Monahan was clearly an accomplished athlete and I had to work hard to keep up with him despite him being ten years my senior and burdened by the object. After what seemed an age we reached the churchyard and sprinted towards the South Door. As the door opened and Monahan slipped through, behind us a gigantic silhouette was passing through the lychgate. From its midst the face of evil stared at me. It was the figure from the picture. It was coming towards me and I froze. Then a hand grabbed my collar and a grip of iron hauled me through the door. As soon as I was safe, quick as a flash, Monahan slammed the door and locked it. We both collapsed behind it and for a moment time seemed to stand still. All became calm. We both knew however that on the other side of the door death waited. Death would be patient.

As soon as a I regained my composure, I thanked Monahan profusely. He was a pale imitation of the figure who had come to the Hexagon. It was almost as if the blood had been drawn from him, and only the husk remained.

'I'm sorry to manhandle you, but it was imperative to gain the protection of the Church. I don't think it will follow us in here, we're quite safe.'

I waved his apology away.

'However … despite the fact that we have reached our haven, the fact remains, we have what it wants. It won't give up.'

He glanced down at the table in front of him; a rather distorted, faded metal object in the shape of a large cup with an odd handle projecting from its base lay where he had placed it. I reached out my hand and for the second time that evening he prevented me from touching it.

'I meant what I said, Jack, leave it alone.' He then repeated:

"…Never touch it come what may
Else dearely learne to rew the day"

Believe me, it's good advice.'

He stared at me with a resolve that belied his exhausted state.

'I clearly owe you an explanation, although I think you have pieced together much of the background. But first let's go back to the vicarage, it's just across the churchyard, and get a stiff drink. I think we'll be quite safe if we leave it here in the sanctuary of God's house.' He nodded towards the table, 'I'll lock it away for safe keeping in the vestry cupboard for tonight. Whatever happens it must not leave the Church under any circumstances.'

'You don't mean we are going out there … where it is?'

He must have detected the ill-disguised panic in my voice.

'Good heavens no, we'll go via the underaisle.'

'The underaisle? Oh yes, I remember it was mentioned in the description of St. Martin's in Black's book.'

'Oh Jack you haven't been reading that old fraud's scribble have you?'

'It was all I could find in Wells', I replied rather apologetically.

He chuckled, I think the release of tension did him good.

'Well at least Black was correct; it does exist. There is a small crypt underneath here and at the far end is a passage, built centuries ago, leading to the vicarage. The crypt is by far the oldest part of the church, pre-dating even this building by many centuries, and it has a part to play in our story, so it's an important place for you to see.'

Then he added, mysteriously, 'Most of all it has a very distinguished inhabitant, but more of that later.'

As he said these words the faintest glimmer of a smile flashed across his face. Changing the subject quickly he said:

'I suspect that the tunnel itself was created so that the vicar of the day could hide recusants or other heretics in less religiously tolerant days. No doubt it was an ideal hideaway for contraband too. It's perfectly navigable, although a little dusty. The entrance door is over there.'

He pointed to the far wall of the east aisle where an oak door was set into the stonework, then he picked up the object and disappeared into the vestry. When he returned, he said:

'I think we shall be safe tonight. Its focus is here in the Church, it will not abandon its charge, until it can reclaim it. Anyway, I'm convinced it is a thing of darkness … mostly.'

Monahan opened the door in the east aisle and we descended a narrow flight of stone steps, eventually reaching the crypt. With only the light of our torches to see by, the shadows on the walls and in the dark corners danced ominously around us and visions of the oubliette at Ashcombe began to loom large in my mind. I started to feel anxious again. If the main body of the church seemed old, I sensed that here we had moved even further back to a time when recorded history began to be unreliable. As I looked around the ancient stonework my eyes came to rest on a stone coffin set on a simple plinth. It was clearly of great antiquity, undoubtedly this was the last resting place of the illustrious figure spoken of by Monahan.

'Ah, I see you have found our patron saint.'

The torch light flickered in that dank subterranean room. After the exertions and terror of the evening, the stillness of the crypt and the relative peace it brought meant that, for a moment, Monahan's words did not register. When they did, I realised the enormity of what he said and suddenly there opened up in my mind a pathway back to the dawn of the Christian Church. For a moment I stood there speechless but, before I could say anything, Monahan gesticulated towards a door at the far end of the vault and, as he did so, shapes all around us followed the motion of his arms. Suddenly the crypt was alive again.

At the door he paused and said:

'I'm convinced our friend Thomas sheltered here after Sedgemoor. It's such a perfect place to conceal someone who doesn't want to be found. Perhaps he did so with the help of the vicar, who knows, until for some reason they fell out and, as Christopher said last night, Thomas was betrayed. After all his relationship with the Church was equivocal, to say the least. Anyway something compelling must have called him to the Hexagon, and whatever it was, it finished him.'

The door opened onto a narrow passage about five feet high. Crouching, we made our way. The air was damp and reeked of decay and I wondered how many souls had languished here in fear of their life. To me, it didn't feel like sanctuary but more like the entrance to perdition. With much relief we reached another door, behind which was the vicarage cellar. We climbed more steps, passed through yet another door and in a moment we were delivered from the chthonian realm.

IX

The Manse was a comfortable house and on such an evening especially welcoming. Monahan had been a widower for some five years and he relied heavily on a housekeeper from the village to maintain order. We sat, barely able to communicate, in the large kitchen where a stove provided much needed warmth,. My host dived straight for the brandy bottle and pour out two large measures. These we consumed avidly, followed swiftly by another.

It is hard to describe how we both felt. One thing was certain: an invisible but undeniable bond had grown between us: I had known Patrick Monahan for barely twenty four hours, but already I had come to admire him as much as anyone I had ever met. As we sat there in restless exhaustion, each replaying the events of the evening, neither of us could comprehend what had happened. The terror had not left us. There, outside in the blackness of the night, it lay in wait.

I was tempted to ask Patrick for his understanding of what we had witnessed, but I could see that he was mentally and physically exhausted. Above all we needed food and rest. For my part I had begun to form a theory, having seen what we'd recovered as well as the evidence of the crypt, but I was by no means confident and had a thousand questions still to ask. I could see from the appearance of my host that it would have to wait until the morning.

'Mrs. Tuffey has left us a cold supper, I don't know about you, but I think we should eat.' I was glad to see that he was gradually recovering his colour, but still I could detect a searching anxiety in his eyes.

After we had eaten, he disappeared into his study and brought back some papers, which he handed to me.

'Jack, you must have many questions to ask. This might answer some of them; it's not too long but essential for putting events into context. It's the product of research I've been working on but only in draft at this stage, and after tonight's little episode, it will need some revision. Take it to bed with you and hopefully we can discuss everything tomorrow. You never know it may help you sleep.'

When I finally got into bed, I turned my attention to the paper and by the end I realised that I had become embroiled in one of the great stories of the Early Christian Church in England. I started to read:

The Coming of St Ciarán of Saighir

The journey had been a harrowing one, sea voyages in the fifth century were always fraught with danger. The large curragh which bore Ciaran and his small band of missionaries from Ireland, although seaworthy, had been tossed on the water like a cork. At last a wave of relief passed through the whole boat, someone had sight of landfall. Ciaran surveyed his fellow travellers. This was no ordinary gathering, but some of the most notable Irish Christians of their time: there was Breaca, a disciple of St Brigid; Germochus, an Irish King and his mother Wingel, accompanied by a society of nuns. He glanced towards the serious Sinninus, an Abbot of some renown, but of all the august gathering Ciaran concentrated his thoughts on the monk, Martain, a friend since boyhood and the most devout member of the company. Martain, was one of the most respected scholars in Ireland, with a reputation which had spread far and wide. In time all of them were destined to become sanctified in the land that lay before them on the horizon.

Born in the region of Ossory, present-day County Kilkenny and western County Laois, Ciaran and Martain had been raised at Cape Clear Island on the southernmost tip of the Irish mainland. By the time that both Ciaran and Martain beheld the rugged cliffs now coming into view, they were veterans of many voyages. They had made the pilgrimage to Rome and there Ciaran had been ordained as a Bishop. It was as the ship glided towards its destination that he remembered his return from the Eternal City and his momentous meeting with St. Patrick. At that meeting the Patriarch had given him something which Ciaran would bring to a certain place on the Fuaran river and there found his monastery. Ever since it had come into his possession this seemingly insignificant item had exerted a magical influence over him.

But now, despite the material and emotional ties he had to his homeland, the missionary zeal required by the church in Rome was strong. In particular, the fledgling Celtic Church was in a precarious state. Feuding kings and overlords had created an atmosphere of instability such that everything was in a state of impermanence. Ciaran's decision to embark on this journey with his greatest friends was also motivated by more pragmatic concerns. His reputation as a miraculous healer and a perpetrator of wondrous deeds had led to jealousy and antagonism amongst powerful leaders. Fearing that his achievements in strengthening the Church in Ireland might be compromised by his continuing presence, he had decided to join the migration of other Christians and spread the gospel in areas where its influence was tenuous. Little did he realise that his decision to make this journey would be hailed throughout the ages as one of the most important for the early Church in Britain. A legend would grow around his expulsion from Ireland, recounting how local chieftains had flung Ciaran from the cliffs tied to a millstone, from whence he had used this encumbrance to sail to his present destination.

Now, as the boat approached the shore Ciaran felt a

heightened sense of anticipation; somehow he sensed that his life hitherto had been a preparation for what now lay before him.

Even as Ciaran stood on the new-found shore, another joined him. This enigmatic figure was tall and angular with a mass of black curly hair, dark searching eyes and a restless body that seemed never to be still. He was young, only just past puberty in fact, but nonetheless he carried with him that indefinable air of confidence.

The story of Ceann Fiáin, or 'Wild One' in English, is as mysterious as the boy himself. One day, some years earlier, when Ciaran was making a pastoral visit, in the company of Martain, to his Diocese of Ossory, the two of them broke away from their duties to walk in the nearby woods, part of the seemingly endless primeval forest that covered much of Ireland in those far off days. They had been going for some considerable time when they heard a noise coming from the thicket nearby and, most unexpectedly, a human figure emerged from the cover. Rather than take flight, the wild creature who stood before him remained quite impassive, all the time fixing his gaze on Martain. The boy, for he was no more than twelve or thirteen, was wraith-like and clad in the most makeshift skin tunic. His whole appearance was so unkempt that they doubted that he had ever washed in his entire life. Despite his degraded state there was a dignity bordering on defiance in the pose adopted by this strange entity. By far the most striking were the black eyes, which stared unendingly at both churchmen and held them in thrall. Ciaran, whose own powers of perception were legendary, felt that here was a formidable presence, one to be respected and perhaps even feared. Martain, for his part, was utterly enchanted by the stranger and, from that moment, an unbreakable bond was forged between the two.

Martain held out his hand to the lad but there was no response, only the continuous gaze which revealed nothing of the state of mind behind the mask. It appeared that the boy had no language whatsoever, apart from a few grunts to convey his feelings. So taken was Ciaran with the plight of this unfortunate that he felt a strange and sudden compulsion to take him under his wing. After some persuasion, communicated through rudimentary sign language, the boy consented to go with them. He assigned Ceann Fiáin to Martain's care in the nearby monastery. But the truth was the boy moved freely in both the Bishop's circle and the friary and so absorbed the habits of civilised society. What a pair they must have made: one a devoted disciple of Christ and his untamed counterpart, a child of nature utterly uncorrupted by human society.

At first, Ciaran's followers had no idea what to make of the discovery. It was impossible to communicate with the boy, apart from the frantic hand signals and gestures which are common to all humanity. He ate like an animal, relieved himself in full public view and possessed none of the conduct that is incumbent upon any member of civilised society. Gradually, through patience and considerable empathy with the boy's plight by those in Ciaran's circle, the rudiments of language and the norms of behaviour were introduced. To many people's amazement, Ceann Fiáin, proved to be a prodigious pupil. He devoured knowledge as one would a banquet, as if hitherto his whole life had been a void waiting for the opportunity to acquire all manner of learning.

Rumours soon spread far and wide of the remarkable boy, so much so that many travelled long distances to get a glimpse of him. In a way, this reflected the views of Ciaran and his circle who viewed Ceann Fiáin as a miracle child, someone who, until his encounter with the Bishop of Ossory and Martain, had been entirely untainted by humankind. Ceann Fiáin had always steadfastly refused to talk about his past and who his parents were, even though he now had the benefit of language. But this refusal only added to the mystique of the boy and enhanced his unique reputation. As this unsullied

*being he became the object of persistent evangelism; many
thought that in Ceann Fiáin there lay the opportunity to
create the perfect disciple of Christ. In this sense he was a
metaphor for the Church's mission to spread the gospel
amongst the unenlightened.*

*So the perceived wisdom was that this wonder of nature
had grown up without being exposed to all the doubts and
cynicism that life in a conventional community would bring.
But here was the most curious thing; despite Ceann Fiáin's
willingness to embrace almost every aspect of human society,
when it came to Christian doctrine his would be counsellors
encountered fearful resistance. The opposition was no mere
refusal; any attempt to guide him to the enlightened path was
met with a hostility that genuinely frightened those around
him. It was not that these were violent outbursts, but the
sudden transformation produced was shocking to behold,
enough to freeze the blood of anyone with the misfortune to be
so transfixed. The hapless teachers said they had never seen
such an expression on any human face, looking into those
savage eyes was to peer into the darkest abyss imaginable.
Some even went as far as to say that Satan himself was present
at such moments, to the extent that they found themselves
doubting their own faith. On such occasions Ceann Fiáin
would extol the delights of a hedonistic life of untamed
Nature, reflecting belief in the Pagan religion, as the ultimate
power in existence, in direct opposition to the constrained life
of the devout Christian. Without exception, all who came into
contact with Ceann Fiáin at such moments felt an overwhelming desire to pray for their own souls, and that of the boy, as
soon as they had quit his company.*

*Both Ciaran and Martain harboured ambitions that one
day they might bring his companion to the true religion, but
for the time being they resisted. Try as they might, they could
not escape the presence of a prodigious, irresistible force, one
that they had unleashed on the world. A crisis began to*

develop when it emerged that many of Ceann Fiáin's greatest critics started to suffer fatal accidents, giving rise to the notion that in some way the boy was responsible.

Such was the latent power of Ceann Fiáin's Pagan creed that its protagonists even started to pose a threat to Ciaran and his adherents. Added to this, rivals of the Bishop within his own Church, jealous of his achievements and the pre-eminent position he forged for himself, sought to exploit the situation by moving against him. Their grievances had been strengthened by the fact that it was Ciaran who had taken in Ceann Fiáin, who seemed no better than a heretic. These challenges weighed heavily on Ciaran. Eventually he called into question his very presence in the land of his birth. Then one night St. Peter, no less, the 'Rock' of the early Christian Church, appeared to him in a dream calling on him to demonstrate his faith by preaching the gospel overseas. The Saint warned, however, of a shadow cast over his voyage and how this would provide a great challenge to be overcome. When he awoke, so powerful had been this vision that Ciaran found his mind was made up. Although he worried privately about a darkness surrounding his enterprise he resolved to embark on missionary work at the earliest opportunity. With all the zeal of the converted he set about preparing for his departure. There remained one dilemma; what would become of Ceann Fiáin?

The answer to this question was resolved quite simply, as his turbulent charge was so keen to accompany him on his travels that he had little choice but to accede to these demands. This despite the cult which was growing up around him in Ireland. So it was that Ceann Fiáin, the mysterious child of Nature and a heretic to boot, sailed with Ciaran, Martain and their doughty band of followers to Cornwall. This voyage would be remembered as the moment when Cornwall's patron saint Piran, as he would be known in Cornish, found the land with which he would become synonymous.

The establishment of St. Piran's Church at Perranzabuloe is well known; what is less familiar is the part played by his companions who carried their ministry further along the coast. It was agreed that Martain would take Ceann Fiáin with him and travel to the marshlands of what is now known as Somerset, where Martain carried one of Christendom's most sacred objects, given to him by Ciaran. Amongst these inhospitable wetlands, the first of what were to be three Churches dedicated to St. Martin, as the anglicised version became, was built. It appears that Martain charged Ceann Fiáin with returning that most precious of all artefacts, its function completed, to Ciaran in Cornwall.

At this point legend takes over. It seems that neither the boy nor his cargo ever reached their destination. What we do know is that Martain died around this time and that Ceann Fiáin remained in Somerset in possession of his prize. One story recounts how the evil which had been latent within him now took over and his infamy became notorious. Although he managed to persuade some easily exploited people to follow him, many went in terror at the mere sound of his name. It is said that he had hidden the Church's holy icon somewhere in the marshes to deprive Christianity of its powers. Eventually his crimes caught up with him; he was taken prisoner and burnt at the stake. His ashes were scattered by his infamous followers at a secret place on the levels. As the flames devoured him he uttered the most dreadful curse on the Church, vowing to keep and stand as guardian over its sacred property, even suggesting that in some way he had 'recovered' the object, saying that no man shall touch it without the certainty of death. At the end, it is said, he screamed 'I am immortal, I shall never die.'

I put the manuscript down. I could see now that HH and Monahan had worked together on the Martaineszoy affair. The discovery of the drawing and the verses had clearly led them to the secret of the Hexagon, but somehow HH had touched this sacred object now possessed by the remains of Thomas Strickland. The rest of Monahan's account gave rise to supposition only. Presumably, the object had been buried by Ceann Fiáin on the mound of Martaineszoy and his ashes were subsequently scattered there. Then, centuries later, along comes Sir Richard de Betancourt who hears the legend of Ceann Fiáin, which has come down to him from the so-called Dark Ages. The story that Martaineszoy is the place where this 'treasure' is to be found excites Richard, always keen to acquire yet more wealth, with the extra convenience that this bounty is on his own land. Subsequently, he searches for and discovers, to his undoubted disappointment, what appears to be a rather tawdry piece of metal. The object, although of immense spiritual value, is of no immediate use to the mercenary knight and, as Christopher revealed on the previous evening, he leaves it in place.

It is, perhaps, appropriate at this moment to consider the psychology of a man like Richard; he is in possession of an artefact which carries with it a curse and a power to those who possess it. Here it is worth considering, too, how suggestible the population were in the fifteenth century; all manner of miraculous deeds and ideas could be ascribed to people and objects at a time when faith, not science, was the catalyst for belief. I knew from the papers found in the desk at Ashcombe that Sir Simon recounts the terror exerted by Richard, so it is reasonable to assume that he exploited it for all he was worth. One can only guess at the fear this evil man spread and what crimes it helped him carry out. One thing is certain, on the strength of this discovery Richard builds the Hexagon and, in doing so reinforces the already cursed reputation of Martin's Hill. As I turned these ideas over in my head, I began to regret even more the loss of the papers written by Richard to which Sir Simon had made reference, if only the old knight had not destroyed them, they would have told us a great deal. What I could say beyond conjecture, however, is that the fault line in the de Betancourt genes, spoken of by Sir Simon with such anxiety, begins with Sir Richard and the legacy of Ceann Fiáin.

My only question was one of chronology. Richard apparently died in the year after the murder of Cavendish at Ashcombe, so I imagine the discovery of the Ceann Fiáin's 'treasure' must have been earlier in his life. Christopher, in his remarks, had put the date of the Hexagon at around 1450 and this seemed entirely feasible. I pictured Richard as a man reinvigorated by his new-found power leading him on to untold depravity. This was the moment when his notoriety was born. One thing remained certain: the picture and its poem are contemporary with Sir Simon and reflects the story of the Hexagon to that date.

I continued to theorise. Two centuries later, Thomas Strickland, no doubt secretly primed by his mother Matilda, also discovers the object and somehow recognises its power. Thomas, who is open to all manner of heretical belief, immerses himself in the satanic possibilities which the object seems to offer, and revels in the presence of a six-sided shrine to the Devil. One imagines that he and his followers were immune to the curse because of their sympathy with the cause of Ceann Fiáin. I suspect that his appalling fate had nothing to do with the legend; rather it was just a case of his past catching up with him and, of course, supporting the wrong side in the Monmouth Rebellion.

The more I speculated the more I realised that there was much I still could not understand, not the least of which was just what the object was and how it has come to possess what seem to be demonic powers. There was little doubt that I would have to wait for the morning and hear what Patrick had to say.

I put down the paper and went to the window. The restlessness of earlier had quite died down and a bright moon shone on the churchyard. Yet somehow a presence remained. It was there in the trees, among the gravestones and at the gate. Much as I wanted to deny it, I knew deep down that the horror would return, sooner or later.

It was sooner.

There crouching by the lychgate was the figure. Its face was turned away from me as if fixed on the west door of the church. I watched with morbid fascination, as his head turned so that the hideous apparition was staring straight at me. It was a pitiless, malevolent gaze without the slightest suggestion of compassion, I was convinced that its entire being was generated by one thing and one thing only, pure wickedness. The shape started to move towards me making its way through the lychgate and towards the vicarage. A cold sweat ran down my back and a shiver gripped my whole body. My tormentor rose up and its form filled the window, shutting out the moonlight. For what seemed an age the cadaverous face glared at me with utter disdain, all the time hypnotising me with unrelenting eyes. Then, a movement, as if it would pass through the windowpane itself and into my room. A terrifying smile passed over the dreadful countenance; it was the ultimate parody of humour, a distortion of all that was wholesome. I sensed that a moment of crisis had arrived and yet I felt helpless to resist. Without warning and for what appeared to be no reason, the phantom … disappeared.

But the eyes remained.

All through the whole affair it had been eyes that haunted me; it began with HH's eerie stare and now I had looked into the very same eyes which no doubt he had seen at the point of death. Disembodied, soulless windows into a world of unimaginable darkness. I knew that I had to tear myself away or suffer the consequences and, with a herculean effort, I closed the curtains. I was in such a state of terror it was all I could do to grope for the bed and collapse into a fitful torpor. There I lay all night expecting to see the towering figure from the Hexagon, while all the time those merciless eyes transfixed me.

When I woke the next morning I felt as though I had not slept for eons, my whole body drained. Even now as I closed my eyes those of the figure would materialise, possessing every part of my being. Desperate for company I dragged myself down to breakfast. As much as I was able, I recounted the traumas of the night to Patrick, who in stark contrast to my own exhausted state looked refreshed by his night's sleep. He had seen nothing, but what I had to say clearly upset him.

'I should never have dragged you over to the Hexagon,' he said full of remorse.

'No, please don't reproach yourself. HH wanted me involved and I'm beginning to see why, in some way, first at Ashcombe and now at the Hexagon, I seem to act as a catalyst for events. Without any arrogance I think I can say that my involvement in Sir Simon's little game would appear to be critical.' I replied.

I raised my hand as if to indicate my desire to move on …

After two large cups of black coffee I felt able to discuss matters with a clearer head. Besides which there were many things I still did not understand and I was anxious to hear what he had to say. I outlined my thoughts on his paper and was relieved to hear that Monahan largely agreed with the conclusions I had drawn.

'Let me now fill in the blank spaces for you, as far as I know them,' he said. 'You're right; poor Harry touched the object in question and came to me suggesting that what we suspected was indeed correct. You see, the history of the Irish saints and their voyages to England was the subject of my doctoral thesis at Trinity. As soon as Harry discovered that picture and worked out the verses, I realised we were onto a major discovery. I let him investigate, something that I bitterly regret now. He was so clever; having known the Hexagon throughout his life, all he needed was the wording of the verses to work out its secret. So he set about dislodging a stone or two, and the rest you know.

'When he died I was certain that because he did not wear a cross he was not protected from the evils that now surround St Patrick's Bell.'

I was dumbfounded.

'St Patrick's Bell? You mean to say that tarnished relic we rescued is really *the* handbell which Patrick is supposed to have given Ciaran, or Piran as I know him.'

'It is the very same,' he said with some conviction, 'not that you will hear it ring, the clapper has long since gone.'

'Oh, I've heard it alright.'

'You poor soul, I am so sorry. How bad has it been?'

'Bad enough. But please carry on, that's the most important thing now.'

He could see my reluctance to talk about it, so after a suitable pause he began again.

'The fact that this is St. Patrick's Bell alone would make it one of the most sacred objects of Christendom. But wait until you hear what my research shows.'

'I'm all ears, tell me.'

'Well, the first thing to understand is that the Bell was given to Ciaran so that he might ring it wherever he wished to establish a church. He used it first in Ireland beside the Fuaran river to found his monastery there, and again, of course in Cornwall. The Bell, when used by the faithful, was a guarantee that the church on that site would endure. Well, it certainly seems to have worked in the case of Martaineszoy. Our Lord declared that Peter was the rock on which the Christian Church was founded and since then bells have always been an integral part of every church. How else were the faithful to be called to worship.

'By the way, you say in your paper that Ceann Fiáin "recovered" the Bell,' I said. 'I don't understand, I thought he was the one who had stolen it.'

'Some years ago I discovered ancient papers in the ecclesiastical archives in Dublin. The irony of all ironies is that the document hinted at the fact that the Bell was originally discovered in Ireland as a pagan artefact, imbued with all manner of ungodly powers. But it seems that the Bell was taken to Rome and there held up as a symbol of the triumph of light over darkness. For centuries, the Church channelled its powers for the benefit of Christianity but, and it's a big but, the legend says that, should it fall back into the hands of those who created it, all the spiritual force for good would be lost and the powers of evil would hold sway. As we know, it fell into the hands of the mysterious Ceann Fiáin, whose mission seems to have been to recover the Bell. Whatever the truth of it, it's clear that Ceann Fiáin buried it in Martaineszoy as an act of revenge against the Church and his followers cast his ashes there so that he could guard it. As you say Jack, Thomas discovered the Bell, in what circumstances I don't know. Whether he understood its significance or not, he clearly felt that Martaineszoy was a site of some 'spiritual' importance. Somehow or other he and his followers got to hear about the Ceann Fiáin story and Martaineszoy became a 'sacred' place for them. Ceann Fiáin's defence of this pagan symbol was seen by Sir Simon as a 'stand', hence his wording of the verse which both you and Harry deciphered. To such an entity as Ceann Fiáin, burning him at the stake had no effect, it merely produced a change from one form of matter to another, from flesh to ashes. It could never prevent his need to possess the Bell. Last night you and I were witnesses, if I can put it like that, to Ceann Fiáin's attempt to rescue the Bell for the second time.'

'Ah yes, that it explains it, thank you,' I said, 'no doubt Sir Simon had the drawing made specifically to further his purpose in constructing the puzzle.'

'Probably, but as Martaineszoy was part of the de Betancourt lands there may have been a drawing already in existence which he could take advantage of. I guess we will never know for certain.

'Last night I took back possession on behalf of the Church under the protection of the cross, and I hope that will be an end of the matter. As for poor Thomas, I suspect one of his followers managed to ensure somehow that he be 'buried' with the bell, even though he or she probably had to go along with the gesture being a mockery of Thomas, as you surmise. I suspect Geoffrey Vesey, apparently Thomas's closest collaborator, as being the protagonist who ensured the survival of the Bell at Martaineszoy. Like Thomas, he was a rich landowner given over to the dark arts, whose malevolent shadow was never far from Thomas's side. I think he was the only one of Thomas's coterie to survive, and he fled to America soon after Thomas's demise. Whose idea the actual 'burial' site was and how it was kept secret remain a mystery; perhaps the deed was carried out on behalf of the authorities, both Church and State, by mercenaries who were sworn to secrecy on pain of death and who subsequently disappeared from the scene. I suspect the powers that be did not want it known that this was Thomas's 'grave' for fear of creating a shrine. Anyway, whoever's idea it was to place him there, it certainly smacks of a dark irony. In the event, nearly all of Thomas's followers were dead and ordinary folk had no desire to go near the place. So there he remained.

'That leaves the curious last verse of Sir Simon's little poem. It is clearly about Ceann Fiáin and the efforts to convert him to Christianity. I'm sure Sir Simon was unaware that in creating the challenge he had set a trap for the unwary. But it does beg the question, where did our venerable scholar get his information about Ceann Fiáin from? I think it must have come from the Library at Ashcombe and in particular the documents compiled by Richard, but, like so much in this affair, we cannot know for sure. But I do agree with you, what a dreadful pity it is that

Sir Simon saw fit to destroy the evidence. I suppose he was so shocked by what he had read that he felt compelled to remove it once and for all. Most unlike a scholar to do a thing like that but I suppose we judge from our perspective; they were different times. The problem is you cannot stop rumour and presumably the legend ran through the generations of de Betancourts and was repeated by Matilda to her son, hence the arousal of Thomas's interest.

'Anyway, that is my theory which I hope I can now publish in due course. It will cause great controversy, of course, but you and I have had first-hand experience of the power the Bell possesses. As you will have seen, I did not mention the bell by name in my paper. It was written before Harry's discovery and I did not like to tempt fate by being explicit. As you now know, Harry was most insistent that if anything should happen to him that I was to wait for you to come to Somerset. Perhaps it was the de Betancourt connection, I don't know. Whatever the reason, he told me that from the moment he visited the Hexagon, he was never alone.'

He seemed relieved to have unburdened himself.

'It's hard for me to disagree with your analysis', I said, 'but the problem for both of us is that we are at the threshold where scholarship ends and imagination takes over. At least you have some primary sources to support part of your theory, which always helps.' I said.

'You're right, of course, to be cautious and I'm sure Harry would say the same if he were here. How we both miss him and shocking for you to be the one to find him.' He looked at me piteously as he said these words.

'Yes, I miss him …'

My voice broke away and for a few moments we stood in silent contemplation of all that had gone before. Then in sudden shift of emphasis, he said:

'Thank God you didn't touch it, Jack.'

I nodded. 'Well, thanks to you I didn't.'

126

I felt a cold sweat break out on my forehead as I contemplated the consequences of that.

Almost as an afterthought he added, 'Oh, there is one more thing. During my research into Ciaran and Martaine, I came across an alternative name for Ceann Fiáin on several occasions.

He stopped and seemed reluctant to continue.

'What was that?' I asked.

'Well, it was … Ainchríost … the Antichrist.'

There was silence again, no response was necessary. It was some moments before he spoke again.

'"Many deceivers have gone out into the world, those who do not confess that Jesus Christ has come in the flesh; any such person is the deceiver and the antichrist" … as John tells us.' His voice was frail, in direct contrast with the enormity of what he had said.

He was contemplative now. 'Funny thing, I spend my life trying to bring comfort and peace to people's lives and yet the Creed I preach is based entirely on the irrational – the Virgin Birth, The Miracles and, of course, The Resurrection. However much you spend time trying to explain that these events are metaphors or whatever, there is still a dichotomy there: the credibility gap that the Church wrestles with every day. It's events like last night that, ironically, restore one's faith. There *is* a fight to be won, isn't there?'

The last question was almost a supplication. I hardly knew how to respond.

'I think we are all spiritual to a greater or lesser extent. Even an inveterate unbeliever like me, acknowledges the metaphysical. After all, I have first-hand knowledge of it. In our everyday lives we need that which transports us to another world beyond our understanding. For many the thought of an alternative to the humdrum reality is what keeps us sane.'

'Perhaps …' he replied.

I wondered whether events had brought on a crisis of some kind because he now seemed drawn into himself. As quickly as I could, I changed the subject.

'What next, then?'

It was fully a minute before he responded.

'Heretic or not, I must arrange for Thomas to be properly interred; I'm certain Harry would have wanted that, and Christopher too. I presume the Hexagon will be surveyed, recorded and repaired. Whether the family will give permission for a dig there is debatable, given what's happened. I do at least have a proposal for the bell, however, which seems to me to be the most apt solution of all. Last night you saw the stone coffin and heard my somewhat melodramatic announcement. Well, eighteen months ago, when some repairs were being carried out, we discovered the tomb near the perimeter wall of the church adjacent to the crypt. It almost certainly dates from the fourth or fifth century – we had the bones it contained dated professionally – and it must have contained someone of importance, as stone coffins were only reserved for eminent people. I am convinced that they are the remains of our Saint, Martin. I believe I told you that the present church is at least the third on this site, so it is perfectly feasible for him to be buried here. A priest's rosary, or the remains of one, was found with him, so it is a pretty strong chance that it is him. I propose that we place the bell in the coffin with him; it seems to me that it is far too dangerous to display somewhere lest someone should touch it. I cannot take that risk. But once it is restored to its rightful keeper the curse will no longer apply. Assuming, of course, that it remains in place. After that has been done I will inform the bishop, quite irregular but, given the circumstances, I think he will agree it is best course of action.'

'Yes, it seems fitting and the fewer people who know where it is the better.' I replied.

'That brings me, conveniently, to one final task. I wonder whether you would be interested in being present when the Bell is returned to Martaine once and for all. I will ask my curate Geoffrey Anscomb to be there too, but it seems to me that on such a happy occasion more than one person should bear witness to the event. I will, of course, be the only one to handle the Bell, but it would mean a lot to me if you were there. Let's face it Jack, you have given so much to ensure that this moment can happen, it must be right that you see it through to its conclusion. What do you say?'

There was an earnestness and a passion in his voice.

'Thank you. How could I say no after an invitation like that? It must be something about the Irish brogue that is hard to refuse!' I said.

He laughed. 'I had no idea I was so persuasive; I shall remember that for future reference.'

'When do you propose that this ceremony should take place?'

'Well, Geoffrey will be back later this afternoon so shall we say this evening? In the meantime let's have some lunch and then a walk'

'Sounds good.'

X

The day passed pleasantly. After lunch we struck out on a long walk across the Levels; not surprisingly we decided to avoid heading in the direction of the Hexagon. Only once did I catch sight of it at the beginning of our walk, it glowered in the dim light, defiant as ever, blacker than the darkest night. As it came into view Patrick whispered softly.

'I returned there this morning and replaced the stones we dislodged last night as best I could for the moment.'

I was astounded. 'You mean you went there alone … why on earth didn't you tell me?'

'I went before you were up and don't worry I was wearing the cross.'

'It didn't seem to bloody well help last night though, did it?

'We're still here aren't we?' He seemed hurt by my injunction.

'Forgive my language I just fear for your safety, that's all.'

'I know, I know Jack, let's forget the subject and not spoil our walk.' He raised his hand and we spoke no more of it.'

Our walk took us a long way into the heart of this singular terrain but, no matter where we went, the criss-cross of rhines was present. These features gave birth to this landscape, they created the farmland which gives the farmer a livelihood and encouraged others to settle here. As I took all this in I found myself in awe of the men who created these massive drains without the aid of modern machinery. There was a part of me too, that regretted their construction and the loss of natural habitat that ensued. As if to empha-sise what had been lost, here and there we encountered fragments of the original marshes and on these oases wildlife in its many forms thrives. Soon we arrived at Sedgemoor and, as I always do when I visit the site of a battlefield, I tried to imagine myself as being present on that fateful day when the future of the country was held in the balance. These now tranquil acres had been the scene of such carnage, bringing an abrupt and brutal end to many lives and effectively sealing the fate of Sir Thomas Strickland. It was as if I could hear the cries of men in their death throes or watch them fleeing the field in terror only to drown in the sucking bogs that lay in wait for the unwary. It seemed to me that these visions arose from the very fabric of this place, a part of the land's collective memory. Especially so with these meadows, where the mist hangs heavy and the distant views obfuscate; such places are haunted. I felt surrounded by old ghosts, of long dead kings and nobles, of soldiers and ordinary men, ghosts which were still unquiet.

We had hardly spoken during the whole time we were out, just the odd word of explanation from Patrick as we came across certain features. Not that this was evidence of any animosity between us, quite the opposite, but nonetheless, I sensed that Patrick was preoccupied. The restoration of the Bell was the culmination of his life's work so far and it weighed heavily on him. What he said next betrayed as much.

'Even if few will hear of it, today is an important day for the church, I feel honoured to be the instrument by which such a deed will be done. Do you know what worries me most? It's not what we shall do today, which will be a joy, it is the inevitability that the day will arrive when the Bell becomes public knowledge and the whole circus that will inevitably follow. I fear then the Bell will become solely an historical object and not a symbol of the enduring power of the cross.'

'I fear my profession is very guilty in that respect.' I offered apologetically. 'I think it has something to do with people's desire not just to read about the past but have some tangible evidence of its existence.'

'And therein you lies the gulf between you and me. Empiricism and faith; the eternal dichotomy. Do I understand that now you have experienced the supernatural, it really does exist?'

'A part of me that believes that what we 'saw' last night and the encounter in the oubliette at Ashcombe are projected memories dredged up from the depths of my psyche. Who is to say what is real and what is not? You see we both pursue 'truth', whatever that much vaunted term might mean to both of us. It's just that, in your case, inquiry becomes inextricably bound up with faith, so that beyond even truth, objective fact or empiricism, faith still remains. For me, the pursuit of knowledge and the conclusions I draw from it are an end in itself. To stray beyond that removes all the foundations of my reasoning.'

'So we can't expect your imminent conversion to Christianity then.' He was laughing now, so I treated his last remark in the spirit of the moment as playful rhetoric and did not respond.

We arrived back at the vicarage to be greeted by Geoffrey Anscomb. He was, in many ways, the opposite of Patrick, short and earnest, with a quick way of speaking. Despite this there was a warmness about his manner and an ability to convey a respect for others. After tea Patrick took the opportunity to brief him about the extraordinary events of the last twenty four hours. He listened with increasing incredulity to the narrative, but at no time did he contradict the course of action proposed by his senior. Between them they decided that proceedings should be carried out in formal clerical dress as if it was a service of the day. Cassocks and surplices were donned, and we made our way into the church.

Patrick had wrapped the Bell in an embroidered cloth and with some solemnity he raised it up and we followed him as he made his way down the narrow steps to the crypt. Anscomb held a lighted candelabra which enhanced the ritualistic atmosphere of the proceedings. Yet again the shadows swayed in that dark place as if liberated by the candles' light, and the weight of ages bore down on all three of us. It seemed that this incredible affair would be brought to its conclusion with this bizarre ceremony. It is hard to imagine anything quite like it ever having taken place before, even in the long and tortured history of the church.

Patrick signalled and I prepared to open the coffin. After a little effort I was able to push the lid to one side. That was when it happened. In that dark and windless place an unnatural gust took my hair and for a few brief seconds I was disorientated. A warm, unwholesome breath caressed my face like a tentacle seeking a hold. I glanced at Patrick and Geoffrey who remained unmoved and in a trice normality was restored. Despite their stoicism I sensed the presence of evil, even in that most hallowed of places. It might cower in the shadows, but it was there nonetheless, waiting, impatient, malevolent. A part of me now just wanted this over and done with, and, with some relief, I realised Patrick was approaching the stone chest uttering the words of a benison. Slowly and respectfully he placed the Bell in the coffin and, for the first time in perhaps fifteen hundred years, the devout scholar who had journeyed here as a missionary was reunited with one of the most precious relics in Christendom. I glanced down at the contents of the coffin; all I could see in that dim light were a few bones and the remnants of a skull. It was, despite my agnostic tendencies, a poignant moment: to be reminded that no matter how exalted in life we become, death reduces us all to the same state.

The stone lid was replaced and with much relief we made

our way back to the vicarage and not, I'm pleased to say, via the underaisle. Whatever lurked among us in that crypt did not rise up again, but somehow I could not shake off a deep feeling of foreboding. None of us spoke of it afterwards. As we recovered from the emotion of the occasion, Patrick seemed positively transcendental. The joy he felt at achieving the recovery of the Bell overflowed and even suppressed my own misgivings for a while.

'Well, Jack at least one of Sir Simon's tasks is now complete, that must make you happy,' he said.

'Yes and thank you for what you have done today. But of course there is the question of the Bible; remember, it mysteriously disappeared after Simon's death. How on earth do I set about finding that?'

'I sense that you will find a way, believe me. But now is not the time to dwell on that because I have a particularly good bottle from Donegal that needs attention. Geoffrey do stay for supper; I know you are partial to a drop of fuisce. For you heathens, that's our native word for whiskey!'

The three of us spent a rather bibulous and thoroughly enjoyable evening, so much so that the next morning my head was struggling to catch up with the rest of me. There being very little more to be done, I took my leave and we vowed to keep in touch. Patrick was one of those spirits, like Simon, encountered rarely in life. We had shared an incredible experience and, as such, there would be a bond between us for ever.

I returned to Christopher's house and relayed the events of last night to him. He concurred with Patrick's idea about a re-burial for Thomas and would pay all the necessary expenses, to ensure that it was done with due ceremony. Ever the man of the world, he was sceptical about what we had witnessed. Privately, I suspect he thought that the pair of us had overactive imaginations. When I left, Jessica walked to the car with me and as I was about to leave she said:

'Don't worry about Christopher, a lifetime in the Diplomatic Service has made him sceptical about everything. For what it's worth, Jack I know that your account is accurate.' Then a dark expression came across her face; she gripped my arm and said:

'You've heard it too haven't you? The ringing I mean. You know of course that this is far from finished, don't you.'

I nodded and she bade me farewell. Two kindred spirits who needed no further words. I had little doubt that before the whole de Betancourt affair was over we would meet again.

As I drove back to Oxford I was full of conflicted thoughts. Jessica's last words had troubled me, there was no doubting that. She had struck me as someone who was acutely sensitive to matters subliminal; it's what made her playing so special. What she said had stirred in me a deep feeling of unease which had been gnawing at me ever since I left the vicarage. There was little doubt that we were dealing with forces of inestimable power.

With Em due back tomorrow, I needed to stifle my apprehension. I didn't want the shadows within me to intrude on her homecoming.

The day of Em's return were full of stories about New York and the people she had met. I had quite forgotten that when she had left for the States before seeing the pictures so when I brought them out and laid them before her she was thrilled to see them, inspecting each one carefully. Like me, she remarked what a generous bequest it was, until, that is, I placed the picture of the Hexagon in front of her. It was the first time I'd had the courage to look at it since the whole affair had ended. Her face blanched and I thought for one moment she would faint.

'What on earth is the matter?' I asked.

'I never thought that I would see that ghastly drawing ever again.' She could barely get her words out.

'You've seen it before?' I said, incredulous.

'It … it used to hang in the library at Ashcombe.'

For a moment, my whole body was numb, I no longer existed in the present, but instead was transported back to that incredible place and the events of two years ago.

'We all hated it so much that father was forced to get rid of it. I don't know what he did with it, but it is many years since I set eyes on it. Please get rid of it, there is evil there I'm sure.'

It was then that I told her the whole story of my visit to Martaineszoy, the verses, Thomas Strickland, Ceann Fiáin and, of course, HH's part in discovering Sir Simon's document. This redoubled her resolve: under no circumstances was it to remain in the house. The next day I gave it to the person in charge of curating College valuables with instructions that it should be placed in storage out of sight. He reacted somewhat warily to my request but complied, nonetheless.

Two weeks later I received a letter that jolted me to my very core. It was from Geoffrey Anscomb, and read:

The Curate's House
Martaineszoy
Somerset

Dear Dr. Tregarden,

This is one of the most difficult letters I have ever had to write. Please forgive me.

It is with deep sadness that I must inform you of the tragic death of Reverend Monahan. You will be aware that he had been making arrangements for the interment of Thomas Strickland following the restoration of the bell to the grave of our Saint a fortnight ago. As to the former, I shall be officiating at that ceremony next week, but it is while dealing with the latter that Patrick's death occurred. As you know, the placing of the Bell was a great relief to him and for those precious few days after our little ceremony he was buoyant, like a man reborn. Since you left he has been in the habit of checking both the grave and, I'm sorry to say, the Hexagon, every day, hardly surprising given the circumstances. Well, two days ago while ensuring that all was quiet at the Hexagon he tripped, bumped his head and somehow snagged the chain of his crucifix on the door latch. His injury appeared to be only slight but the chain itself was damaged and the crucifix unwearable, so Patrick took it to the jewellers in Taunton for repair. That night for the first time since his ordination he was without the protection of the cross on which our saviour died.

The following morning Mrs Tuffey, his housekeeper, found him sitting bolt upright in bed, obviously dead. The poor soul sent for me straight away although subsequently the shock has taken a heavy toll on her. I shall never forget the scene that greeted me. It was bad enough that this should happen, but what really disturbed me was the awful look on his face. It was as if he had suffered a catatonic fit, but this was no vacant expression, this was a countenance of fear, unadulterated terror, nothing less. The eyes especially will haunt me for the rest of my days. I believe the preliminary findings of the doctor attending were that he had a heart attack perhaps due to delayed reaction to his fall. It is not for me to question the opinion of a doctor, but I don't believe that for a minute, I think you and I might beg to differ.

Two things trouble me greatly – all the doors and windows in the vicarage were either locked or closed, as was the door to the Church, but I found the door to the underaisle open. It is invariably kept shut. I noticed too, that Patrick's Bible was by his bedside open at 2 John 7. You may be familiar with the passage:

"For many deceivers have gone out into the world, men who will not acknowledge the coming of Jesus Christ in the flesh; such a one is the deceiver and the antichrist."

I cannot begin to imagine what took place in that room, but the mere thought of it fills me with horror.

I have this morning summoned the courage to inspect the tomb of our Saint. Remarkably, St. Patrick's Bell remains where it was placed. Thank goodness.

Patrick Monahan was the finest man I have ever known and many of us here will struggle to recover from this tragedy.

I am so sorry to have to write such a letter. This dreadful incident only happened yesterday, but I will let you know the arrangements for the funeral as soon as they are made.

Yours with much sorrow,
Geoffrey Anscomb

I put down the letter and went to the window. In the west the sun was setting over the spires of the colleges, but I looked beyond them to much further afield, where a cheerless ruin stood on a hill amid a windswept plain. I thought of intrepid missionaries long ago who were never to see their homeland again, who had brought with them an object so cherished that, for centuries, possession of it was everything to men. I thought too, of the existence of a world parallel to our own where the laws of nature have long been forsaken. In that realm there exist only the souls of the restless whose essence knows only unquietness. We fill our lives with the endless pursuit of truth, the need for a certainty of belief and the desire for love, all distractions which keep the darkness at bay. The shadowy curtain between these dominions is rarely undrawn. Some of us are destined to glimpse beyond the veil, but it is by no means a privilege to do so.

But most of all I thought of two men: one who had been my mentor since college days and the other I had scarcely known at all, and for the first time in years I wept uncontrollably.

The Librarian

Part One of the Tregarden Ghost Trilogy ...

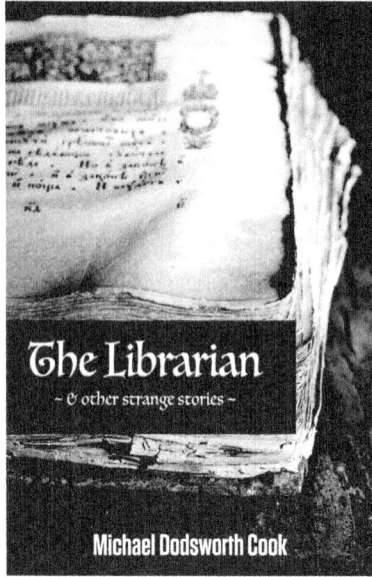

The young Jack Tregarden is befriended by the charismatic Simon de Betancourt at Oxford. Some years later he visits Ashcombe Abbey, the home of the de Betancourts, to catalogue the extraordinary library there. As he begins work he is confronted by a centuries old puzzle and unimaginable forces, which will change his life forever.

Three haunting ghost stories follow:

'24th June'
'How the Trees Grew'
'Golgotha Heights'

Printed in Great Britain
by Amazon